Anne Keens was born in Surrey. From a young age, she had one ambition and this was fulfilled when she trained to become a nurse. After meeting her future husband in Surrey, she then moved with him to his home county of Dorset. Life here revolved around raising her young family and furthering her nursing career. Now with over thirty-five years of nursing experience, Anne is enjoying retirement.

It was a newly found hobby to try creative writing. *When Time Sleeps* is her first novel.

I would like to dedicate my novel to a beloved sister,
Daphne May.

Anne Keens

# WHEN TIME SLEEPS

AUSTIN MACAULEY PUBLISHERS™

LONDON • CAMBRIDGE • NEW YORK • SHARJAH

A CIP catalogue record for this title is available from the British Library.

ISBN 9781788232975 (Paperback)
ISBN 9781788232944 (ePub e-book)

www.austinmacauley.com

First Published (2021)
Austin Macauley Publishers Ltd
25 Canada Square
Canary Wharf
London
E14 5LQ

Thank you to my wonderful family for their
support and encouragement.

# Prologue

The dark shadow of a figure, standing at the foot of the bed, begins to move. It walks slowly towards me and as it reaches my side, bends over me. Upright again, I watch as it turns and walks across the room and disappears through the wall...

# Chapter 1

## The Beginning

I don't want to wake up yet; I'm feeling certain that I have only just dropped off. My head is throbbing and my limbs ache. Blinking my sticky eyes open and focussing on my surroundings, the room appears to be shadowed in darkness. I'm lying on the couch, so I must be in the lounge. What time can it be? Turning my head slowly towards the clock, I can see it shows twenty-five past twelve. Lifting my head from the cushion is far from easy. My mind is in a state of confusion as I try to remember what has happened to make me feel this way. The misty gauze, that seems to cover my brain, will only let a few recollections through; and I struggle to piece together enough information to help bring me back to full comprehension. As the clock chimes for the half hour, I realise that I have only been asleep for forty minutes. Looking out through the window, I notice the dark clouds filling the skies. Suddenly, a flash of lightning startles me, it is quickly followed by a rumble of thunder. Saliva is beginning to moisten my dry mouth and I swallow hard. Trying to compose myself, I begin to recollect the reasons for my feelings of such anguish and despair. Tears come easily again and I begin to sob; shallow rapid gasps with the occasional sharp intake of a deeper breath. I am unable to stop myself until the tightness in my chest and an ache in my ribs brings me back to some measure of control.

"Jamie, why did you leave me?" I cry out, "It's just not fair!"

Cancer is such a cruel disease. It is evil, destructive and difficult to fight. If only Jamie had made that appointment and gone to see the doctor sooner. Perhaps then he may have had a chance! After all, not everyone dies from cancer; at least not without a fight. His excuse was always that he had been too busy.

"There is always next week," he would say.

Why did I not nag him? After all, I would nag him about other things that now seem trivial by comparison. In hindsight, I wish I had gone behind his back and made the appointment for him myself. I had witnessed more often, in his last few months, that Jamie's cough had seemed a lot worse. He would rub his chest with his fist.

"It's only indigestion!" he would say, "It'll be gone in a few minutes."

Often he took over-the-counter remedies to help ease the pain. I noticed that this was happening more frequently. Only following a particularly bad night, when the pain kept him and I awake for most of the night, did he then, finally, pick up the phone to make an appointment to see the doctor. He was told by the receptionist that there were no available appointments for two weeks unless he thought that it was an emergency. I was frustrated that he did not think so.

"Anyway, how am I supposed to know whether it is an emergency or not?" he said. "After all, I'm not the doctor, am I?"

I was so angry and wanted to phone the surgery straight back, but he said he didn't want me to make a fuss. A quarrel had broken out between us. Heated words were spoken. What a waste of time this all was!

What were the chances of both of us being given a diagnosis of cancer? Statistically, one in three people are likely to have cancer sometime in their lives. Unlike Jamie, I had experience of this life-threatening disease.

My nursing career, of over thirty-five years, had seen me witness the cruelty and devastation that cancer had bought to some of my patients (and their families). Nursing had been a calling from my early years. On completion of my training, I had chosen to work in the operating department of my local hospital as a theatre nurse. Working along-side skilful surgeons, I saw the effects of cancer on the inside of the body; the ugly growths and tumours invading the healthy tissue of the young and old alike. After a few years, I went to work on the medical wards caring for cancer patients.

Throughout this time, I had been keen to read new medical research articles and would listen with excitement and hope to news broadcasts, whenever there were statements made by medical reporters and health organisations. There has been a great deal of progress made in the earlier detection of some cancers with the use of X-rays, scans and blood tests. Enthusiastic scientists continue to raise the hopes of individuals with their reports of a so-called 'breakthrough' or of a major new treatment or drug. However, they always seem to end their report with a statement of caution: *Although the initial clinical trials look promising, we must appreciate that it will be at least two more years of clinical trials before the new drug can be finally used to treat cancer patients.*

Some of the most well-known treatments for cancer have uncomfortable and debilitating side effects for a lot of people. Any progress made to improve these current treatments, and minimise the side effects, would be greatly welcomed.

I suppose I could say I have been one of the lucky ones, following my early diagnosis from a routine scan. The road to recovery after surgery, which involved the removal of the affected breast and lymph nodes, had been a long one. Treatment before, and afterwards, included both radiotherapy and chemotherapy. There had followed some very dark days; with my mind suffering from severe bouts of depression, while at the same time my body was fighting recurrent infections. I tried to remain positive but knew that statistically, I may not be able to beat the disease and that I might die. However, I got through it with help and support from the specialist cancer care team, Jamie, my family and friends. I have now been cancer-free for nearly two years and I thank God every day for this.

# Chapter 2

My body begins to relax. Looking out of the window, the sky is clearing for now, but there are more dark clouds looming. Turning my face more directly to the window, I can feel the warm sunshine through the glass and it feels good. Better make the most of this as it will probably be short-lived! My body suddenly starts to shiver as the sun disappears behind a large, dark grey cloud. I instinctively reach out for a second blanket to wrap around my shoulders, which sends a sharp pain down my back. Wincing, I move my frame into a more comfortable position. Perhaps I have been lying down for too long and that's why I feel uncomfortable? For a split-second, I feel perplexed, for I cannot remember what time of the year it is.

"How stupid I am," I reprimand myself, "of course I know its winter."

It is December and this has always been my favourite month of the year; advent leading through to Christmas. Although I was not a regular church-goer, mainly due to my work commitments, I did love to attend the Advent Carol Service and to join in with the singing of some of my favourite Christmas Carols. The services, held in our village church of Saint Edmund, boasted a full mixed choir of young and old.

This particular year, the service needed the choir to be more involved than usual, which meant that there would be long pauses during the service when the congregation could sit in candlelight, either to pray or to meditate, while listening to the soft voices of their anthems. The journey to celebrate the birth of Christ had begun.

After the services, Jamie and I would walk home and make some mulled wine together. The first of many jugs we would enjoy, throughout the festive season. We would light a fire and cuddle up on the couch, in front of its warmth, and sip the warm, red, spicy liquid. Together we would make plans for our annual Christmas party, drawing up lists of guests and possible menus. Jamie was in charge of ordering in the drinks and I, with help from the family, would organise the food. Oh, how I enjoyed the excitement and anticipation that the approaching festive season always brought!

Most people seemed a lot happier during the month of December, especially those working in the retail industry; an opportunity to boost their sales perhaps? However, I would never be so naïve as to forget those that do not enjoy this time of year. Many people find it increasingly difficult and cannot wait for it all to be over: the poor or lonely, the sick or bereaved.

I guess I'm one of the lucky ones. Only on a few occasions in my life have there been times when Christmas has been a little more difficult to celebrate. For example, following the loss of a loved one within our family. No one knew better than Jamie, how much the season meant to me. He would often tease me about how it seemed, to him, that he had only just finished putting the decorations back in the attic from the previous Christmas. I especially loved the excitement and anticipation for the big day and would start to prepare very early. The cake was made first, using the family recipe and a feed of brandy added weekly until it was time to ice. This was always a favourite with my family, as was the traditional Christmas pudding, another family recipe.

My thoughts wander back to last Christmas when we had all our family together. This couldn't always be the case as we were busy people, living busy lives. Our daughter, Lottie and I, could not always have the same holidays off work. Careers in nursing meant we had to work shifts. Christmas lunch would sometimes be Christmas dinner. Occasionally, it would be served on Christmas Eve. And sometimes, we would have to delay the meal until Boxing Day. It didn't really matter as we would still enjoy the time we had together.

Our children were now grown-ups and it was time to support those in the profession with younger children at home waiting for their mum or dad to return so that they could open their presents. Jamie and I were so proud of both our children.

When Lottie told us she was considering nursing as a career, we were delighted that she would follow in my footsteps. As a small child, she often played at being a nurse. Her dolls and her favourite teddy, Barny Bear, would be tucked up in her bed. She would bandage them, give them medicine and pretend they would object. To this, she would comfort them and tell them that it would make them feel better. If only I could do this in real life! I think I knew then that one day she would become a nurse like me.

Our son, Mathew, had gone to university to study engineering. On completion of his degree, he had decided to enlist in the army. He had trained hard and had chosen to learn about the mechanics of explosive devices in order to work in bomb disposal. In later years, he worked for army intelligence. He was sometimes secretive about the nature of his work and we understood why. We would always support our children in whatever they did. Some of our darkest days, however, were when Mathew had been deployed to a war zone.

"You know it's my job, Mum," he would say, "I have to go wherever I am needed; wherever they send me."

I prayed like I had never prayed before for his safe return, and God never failed me. And so, we had one of our best Christmas's ever. Our son-in-law, Pete, had helped with the cooking. We were quite spoilt, having a chef in the family. When Lottie first met Pete, he was working in a local pub and she had often suggested that we ate there as the food was so good. It had been at the end of an evening dining together to celebrate Jamie's birthday, that Pete had come out of the kitchen, having completed his shift. He recognised Lottie from school and they exchanged telephone numbers, having first agreed to meet up. That was nearly five years ago. Pete was ambitious and wanted to manage and cook in his own restaurant. He worked hard, attending college at the same time as working as a chef. Both he and Lottie saved hard and it had paid off; Pete was now the owner of a successful small restaurant. Lottie and Pete were married and lived in the flat above the restaurant.

Mathew's girlfriend, Abbie, had also spent Christmas day with us. Her family lived across the border in Surrey and so they shared their time between the two families. We had all gone to Midnight Mass on Christmas Eve, and so we didn't feel too guilty at not attending the morning service. I have such happy memories of that last Christmas. Somewhere from the back of my mind came the words, "God gave us memories so that we might have roses in December." It had been my grandmother who would quote these words, from the author James Barrie, in times of sadness and loss. She was a beautiful and kind lady who I loved dearly.

# Chapter 3

My thoughts were disturbed as the clock began to chime. Even in the darkness of the room, where clouds once again were accumulating in the skies outside, and through teary, swollen and sore eyes, I could see that it was now one o'clock. Why had I then counted two chimes?

"Stupid clock," I said out loud, and then remembered that it does this now and again. I am exceptionally fond of this crazy and strange clock that Jamie and I had bought on a whim.

We were meeting Mathew in London for the weekend. I had bought theatre tickets for his birthday and we had agreed to meet up that evening. Having free time to spare, Jamie and I decided to do a little shop fuddling. Leaving Waterloo station, we had caught a hop-on hop-off bus. We always preferred to use the buses as opposed to the tube trains. You could see more of the city this way, and get off to wander the streets whenever something took your fancy. And so we found ourselves in Putney. We walked for a short time by the riverside and stopped to admire the young athletic men and women in their rowing boats. We always said we would come to London for the Oxford and Cambridge boat race but never had. Afterwards, we wandered into the town, peering into shop windows.

This is where we had come upon the interesting clock shop. Browsing through the window, there had been a selection of some modern, but mostly antique clocks. We had been looking for a replacement one for quite a while as our old mantle clock had suddenly stopped working. We had been told by the clock repairer that it would cost more to fix it than it was worth and that there would be no guarantee that it would not stop again.

We spent more money than we had intended to. I had fallen in love with the nineteenth-century French, glass mantle clock with its beautiful Corinthian, gold-painted columns. It had an eight-day movement, striking on the hour and half-hour on a coil gong. Its workings, on clear view through the glass, were a delight to observe.

That evening, much to Mathew's amusement, we had to carry the clock with us to the theatre, as we didn't have time to drop it off at the hotel. I remember it had been quite heavy, and I had been afraid of dropping it. However, it survived the journey intact and came home with us. A few weeks later, we considered taking it back to the antique shop because the number of chimes had come out of synchronization with the hour of the day. Eventually, however, the clock managed to settle down. The chiming corrected itself, except for the hour of one o'clock, when it continued to chime twice. We had decided that this made the clock unique and we loved it. It had become a talking point and the subject of much amusement during the times when we entertained guests.

# Chapter 4

With my eyes closed, and feeling sleepy, I am suddenly disturbed; aware of a noise, which sounded as if it was coming from behind me, back towards the kitchen. I could hear what I thought were faint mutterings; and then a soft singing voice of a woman, which was intermittent with the sound of humming. I try to rationalise what I can hear. My mind must be playing tricks on me and I conclude that the sounds must be coming from outside the house.

Our property is detached and sits within an acre of land. We are surrounded by fields on one side and beautiful countryside on the other. In the distance, just beyond the fields, it is possible to see the tall chimneys of the large manor house and its vast estate. The tall older trees, and newly planted ones, are creating a splendid forest. From the north side of the house, we boast distant views of the village and can clearly see some of the thatched rooftops and chimneys as well as the tall church spire of St Edmund's. One other property shares the intimacy of our plot. The family in that house have become good neighbours and friends. A short-cut from the bottom of their garden is the closest access to our back garden.

The village is walking distance from our house, for those that enjoy a bit of exercise. The lane, however, is more like a track, with grass growing in the middle and occasional potholes on either side. The type of weather would determine if a person could choose to walk or not. Therefore, most visitors to our home would arrive by some means of motorised transport. I decided that the sounds were most likely coming from people who were possibly out walking and had taken a wrong turn. If they chose to knock at my door today, I decided I would be rude and not answer it.

I am not expecting any visitors as I had requested, firmly, that I wanted to be left alone. On my own, I could mourn in a way that some might construe to be selfish. I didn't care about the feelings of others. Jamie was my loss and mine alone. I knew I would eventually have to be strong for our children, but not at this time. Left on my own, I could cry out loud if I felt like it, and swear at the unjustness and the unfairness of my loss. I didn't want other people to see me like this, or try to offer me comforting words. It was more than likely that I would not be able to be civil towards them, and they may not be able to understand my feelings of anger.

I have been to a number of funerals over the years. Some of these have been for very special and significant people in my life. How many times have I grieved with their families and friends? Assuring them that I would always be there for them should they need me. It's cruel. We all say: "Life is for the living, and must go on." As time goes by, the people we lose suddenly fade from our thoughts as we busy ourselves and get caught up in our own lives. Occasional reminders bring them temporarily back to the fore; a significant date, perhaps a birthday or anniversary, a treasured possession or keep-sake.

The sounds of singing and humming continue. They become a little louder and as I listen more acutely, I realise that I can distinguish some of the lyrics.

"Down in the vale, diddle diddle. Where flowers grow. And the birds sing diddle diddle. All in a row." The tune is vaguely familiar but I can't quite recall where I have heard it before. The owner of the voice can sing well. I want to smile, but I don't know why and I start to hum along softly to the tune.

Turning my head towards the sound, which I can now establish is coming from somewhere behind me, I notice that the door is slightly ajar to the kitchen. In comparison with the darkness of the lounge, there is a brightness there that seems out of place. I have to blink a few times to convince myself that this is really happening and not a dream. Getting up off the sofa, I turn towards the kitchen. My body stands motionless, for I cannot seem to put one foot in front of the other, and I strain my eyes to see what I think is movement behind the bright lights. Suddenly, it starts to become a little clearer, like a thin cloud passing in front of the sun, and I know then that I must be dreaming. In that instance, the door opens slowly, just a few more degrees, and I see what I cannot believe. There is a cow in my kitchen! What the hell is happening to me?

I see the bulk of a young cow. Only its head and body can be seen down to the middle of its brown, muddy legs. Below this, there appears to be a grey mist. I must be dreaming, or hallucinating. Rubbing and blinking my eyes, which are still very sore from crying, does not help. I can still see it. I must be witnessing an apparition. Just like the story I had heard whilst visiting the city of York on one of our holidays.

We had been told by the curator of an old house we had visited that in the year of 1953, a man called Harry Martindale, an apprentice plumber, had been working in the basement of this house. He claimed to have been spooked by an apparition of Roman soldiers. These, he could only see from their knees upwards.

I have always believed in ghosts or visiting spirits. After all, I had occasionally been visited in our bedroom, in the dark of the night, by a tall man wearing a full-length dark coat and a wide-brimmed flat hat. When this first happened, shortly after we had settled into our new house, I had been frightened and begged Jamie to change sides of the bed with me. The ghost of the man always stood motionless at the bottom of our bed, before moving to my side. It didn't seem to matter which side of the bed I had chosen to sleep on as he always seemed to know where I was. Over the years, I began to feel less afraid, and would no longer call out to Jamie. Instead, I would lie still and watch as the man stood at my side and then walk across the room, sometimes appearing to turn towards me for a second glance, before disappearing through the wall.

I remember discussing this with my mother and she had responded by telling me of her own experiences with visiting spirits. She would always tell me not to be scared of seeing ghosts and that they would not harm me. My mother was convinced that they came with messages from the ones we had loved and lost. She would go on to say that she was more afraid of the living than the dead. Where was she now when I needed her? I wondered what she would make of this apparition.

A streak of lightning closely followed by a clap of thunder, briefly takes my attention from the scene in the kitchen to the window on my right. Outside, the rain is lashing down and changes to hailstones that clatter against the windowpane. The sounds coming from the kitchen are getting louder as if competing with the noise that the hail storm is making. Clear voices are shouting.

"Daniel, Daniel, for goodness sake, come quickly, there's another cow in my kitchen. It's happened again!" a woman shouts.

"It's OK, Ma, I'm coming."

I stand motionless, in awe, just feet away from the door. The light within this room is in stark contrast to the room in which I stand. Taking steps forward and progressing cautiously towards the light, I can see the figure of a man trying to entice the cow away, pulling on a rope which is tied around the animal's neck. Then I see a woman at the rear end of the cow. She is trying to encourage the beast to move by striking it across its back with what looks like a pair of old fashioned wooden wash sticks, the kind I have seen in a museum.

Both people are only visible down as far as their knees. They do not appear to notice me watching just a few feet from the door. I can feel my pulse quickening but for some weird reason, which I could not explain, I did not feel afraid. Placing my hand to my mouth, I manage to stifle a soft giggle. I could be watching a scene from a period comedy if there is such a thing. From what I could see, the room appeared to be from another time. Turning my attention to the two individuals, I notice that they appeared to be dressed in clothing from about the 1940s. The woman is wearing a full-length skirt and a knitted cardigan. Her sleeves are drawn up to her elbows. Over the top of her clothes, she is wearing a full apron in a brightly coloured floral print. Her hair is tied up in a scarf, fashioned like the ones I had seen in films set in this era.

The man is wearing what appears to be an all in one boiler suit which has a belt tied around his middle. His sleeves are rolled up and I can see his muscular arms. On his head, he is wearing a flat tweed cap. I feel a sudden desire to see more. These two people, trying to move a cow from what appears to be an old kitchen, unlike my newly built one of recent years, encourage me to go a little closer.

"This is ridiculous," I say out loud, "I must be going mad."

I quickly turn to look around the lounge and confirm that all is as it should be in there. My kitchen, however, was most definitely not!

# Chapter 5

My husband, Jamie, was an architect by profession and had designed our house. He had meticulously followed the progress of the house during its construction. I had begged Jamie to buy the land as it held so many memories for me. My grandparents had lived in one of the two cottages on the property. My mother had been born there and so, I had been told, had I. The land was sold through an auction. It was the only time we had ever been to one of these and therefore we were both inexperienced. The price for the land was more than we had wanted to spend. With my fingers crossed, I waited eagerly for the hammer to come down on our final bid. I truly believed it was meant to be and the land was now ours. We did have to cut back a little when it came to the design of the new house but that did not matter.

Hand in hand with my mother, we had stood and watched as the bulldozer came in to demolish the remaining broken walls of the cottages. It had been an emotional experience for the both of us. Mum had been a very practical sort of person and had lived her life in the current times. She was not one to harp on about the past too often and was always excited by prospects of new challenging experiences; however, we would not have bought the land without her blessing. She was quite excited, watching as the new building took shape. We had plans to include a room for her if she had wanted to live with us, but my independent mother had refused.

"I'm happy where I am, thank you. I like my own company and have lots of friends, should I choose to spend time with them."

Mum's cottage was quite old fashioned but did have all the amenities that were required to live comfortably.

"Well, if you ever change your mind, there will always be room for you here."

She squeezed my hand gently and smiled.

"I know you are always looking out for me and I feel so lucky to have you and the family around me."

The land had an area of what would have been a garden, slightly sloping down towards a field belonging to the Browns' farm. The farm itself was long gone and the field was now rented out privately to a horse owner, for grazing. To the side of the walls were the remains of an old apple-tree orchard. All had been very overgrown. The few remaining apple trees were pulled from their roots and had come out easily. We did, however, decide to plant two new apple trees, as well as pear and plum trees for our own benefit.

I find myself standing at the kitchen door which has approximately a half of its aperture open. The occupants inside do not appear to notice me as I stand in awe of the scene I am witnessing. The cow is mooing with objection as it is being banished from the kitchen. Unable to contain myself any longer, I cautiously edge through the doorway, stepping carefully as I do so, down onto the cold kitchen floor. Standing quite still in the room, I realise that I must be invisible to the two individuals that I have been watching in front of me. It may be my imagination, however, I'm sure the cow just turned its head towards me, giving another loud moo as I take a few more steps nearer.

On closer observation, I'm shocked and astounded, as I quickly realise that the two people are not strangers to me. Drawing in slow, rhythmic, deep breaths, I try to calm myself. My heart is beating faster with the excitement of what I have now realised. Though much younger than I could remember, but from old photographs, I could distinguish that, the woman is none other than my grandmother. The man she had called Daniel, is none other than my father.

Memories come flooding back as I take more notice of my surroundings. I realise that they too are not unfamiliar to me. I remember that the room in which I'm standing in is the kitchen; that formed part of the house that I had once lived in. Why should I be experiencing happy memories from my childhood, which now seem such a long time ago?

"Shoo! Come on now, girl, out of my kitchen," my grandmother shouts. "Look at the bloody mess you're making of my clean floor!"

"It's OK, Ma, she's moving now. Good girl, out you come."

My father leads the animal out through the door opposite and into the yard; the cow mooing in defiance of the indignant way she was being banished from the kitchen.

On the opposite side of the room, I spy the familiar window seat and make my way across the fouled kitchen floor, being careful not to slip on the wet mud. Seating myself down on the faded cushions, I turn around and peer out of the window, watching as my father leads the animal down the path and back to the field where it probably came from. In the distance, I can see more cows in the field. I wonder who had carelessly left the gate open, allowing the animal to escape.

Meanwhile, my grandmother goes about her business and starts to clean up the mess left behind. Her mood is less angry and as she does, she starts to sing again. The song is now very familiar to me, and although she does not hear me, I sing along with her remembering clearly the words that I had sung as a young girl. As the words return to me, I realise that at that time, I had obviously not appreciated the sentiments of, what I now understand to be, more adult lyrics.

"A brisk young man diddle, diddle. Met with a maid. And laid her down diddle, diddle. Under the shade. For you and I diddle, diddle. Now all are one. And we will lie diddle, diddle. No more alone."

Feelings of contentment flood over me and for now I have forgotten my sadness. How I loved my dear grandmother. She was always kind and gentle. As a small child, she would lift me up onto her lap and soothe away my hurt with her songs. I inhale deeply as I remember the beautiful smell of her rose scent. She would always keep a bar of rose-scented soap in her bedroom and would let me use it occasionally to wash myself. I wonder if the pretty rose painted soap dish is still upstairs in her bedroom. It had sat on the dressing table along-side the china washbowl and large water jug, which had formed part of the set. Next to this, she kept a soft hairbrush and mirror. She would sit me on her lap, in front of the dressing table mirror and gently brush my hair. I was allowed to hold her delicate hand mirror as she tied ribbons in my hair. I smile to myself as I recall the chamber pot that was also decorated with the same pattern, which was kept under the bed, and wonder if that is also still there.

"Remember, Rosemary, the potty is just for the night time and only for number ones. If you need to do a number two, then you must go outside to the toilet. You can wake me to come with you if you are frightened of the dark."

As far as I can remember, there had never been a bathroom in the house. We had an out-building, that we called the wash house, which had a separate toilet next to it. Pulling its chain to clean the toilet was difficult and it never seemed to work in one pull. On cold nights, a tin bath was brought into the kitchen, once a week, usually on a Sunday and placed in front of the fire. There we would take turns to bathe. Always the cleanest one first, and that was always me. Every other day, we had to get by with a bowl of water and a strip wash.

"Come on, Rosemary," she would encourage, "wash down as far as possible, up as far as possible and possible last."

Focusing on the kitchen, I can see that it's just as I remember. The large red-brick fireplace with the coal-scuttle on the hearth, the high mantle shelf above, adorned with polished brass and copper objects. A Toby jug, positioned in the centre and a few family photographs complete the tableau. Above the fireplace hangs a large framed photograph of a man, in military uniform, sitting astride a horse. I cannot remember who the soldier is. Only that he fought in the Great War. By the side of the fire sits Granddad's chair. A well-worn, wooden, farmhouse armchair with a high crafted wheel back design. Plump, faded cushions adorn the seat and one is tied to its back. There is a rustic table in the centre of the room; slightly off to one side, with six odd chairs placed around it. Next to the sink and wooden drainer is a small gas cooker.

The only other piece of furniture is a large, dark wooden dresser on which sits the crockery and cooking utensils. Everything had its own place and everything sat neatly in its place.

The stairs on the inside wall led up to two bedrooms. A second set of stairs led, from the smaller of these two to an attic room. This I remember is where, as a child, I had slept. I had loved to sit on the windowsill and admire the views from the window, out across the fields and beyond. Nannie once told me that, on a very clear day, it was possible to see into two other counties, I had thought that this had seemed so far away at that time.

Looking back across the kitchen, I notice the door from which I had come in from; and that it now appeared to be closed. From what I could remember, beyond that door was the best room in the house; the formal sitting room that had been out of bounds to everyone! We were only ever allowed to go into this room on Sundays and 'special' days and then, only when accompanied by an adult. The door was kept firmly closed.

The heart of the house was most definitely the kitchen. This was where we all came together, to share in its warmth and the daily rituals of everyday living. I remember the adults, sitting there on an evening, playing cards and drinking cider. Sometimes Nannie would be sat there, knitting or sewing, there were garments to make and even more to repair. Socks were darned and patches were made to cover threadbare garments. Memories of holding a skein of wool between my hands and over my thumbs, so she could wind the wool into a ball, came back to me.

"Never have an idle hand," she would say to those who said they had nothing to do, and she would always find them something to work on.

Oh, my dear Nannie, I wish you could see me. I would just love for you to give me a hug right now. To tell me that everything will be alright.

# Chapter 6

"Ma, come quickly! I think something is happening," the voice of another woman shouts from up the stairs. The tone of voice is one of anxiousness. My grandmother carefully puts her wet mop back into its bucket and places it next to the sink. She lifts the bottom of her apron to dry her reddened, wet hands and hurries back across the room. Lifting the latch that holds the door in place, she hurries up the stairs. As there is no carpet, I am able to count the stairs as she goes up.

As a young child, if I had woken in the night, having been frightened by a bad dream, I would shout down to her and count the stairs as she came to my aid knowing that with every step she was getting closer to me.

I can hear the sounds of the woman upstairs and she seems to be in distress. Coming down the stairs again, my grandmother hurries to the door and shouts loudly for Daniel to come. From the window, I can see my father at the bottom of the garden. He is digging in the vegetable patch. Dropping his fork, he immediately responds to my grandmother's voice and makes quick progress up the garden path. Running into the kitchen, my father is out of breath.

"What's the matter?" he asks.

My grandmother ushers my father to the sink to wash his hands.

"I think it has started," she tells him as she pushes a towel into his hands.

"The baby can't come yet. It's not time!"

"From my experience, babies will come when they are ready, my lad. Just you get down to Sister Mary's house and tell her to come quickly. On your way back, look out for Pa and if you see him, tell him to come home now!"

The woman calling from upstairs is sounding impatient, "Mum, Mum, come here. Please. I need you now!"

"It's OK, my dear, I'm coming."

I can do nothing but watch and listen. My perception of the situation upstairs is that the woman who was calling out is most probably in the early stages of labour. I think I might be correct in assuming that she is none other than my mother.

In between the sounds of crying, she is begging for the pain to stop.

My grandmother is calm in her response.

"Calm down, my dear," I hear her say. "You have a long way to go yet, save your energy. Just try to breathe through the pain. That's a good girl."

I jump as my father rushes back into the kitchen. He has obviously completed his task with haste. With him is my grandfather and they are both out of breath. How excited I feel as I study them both. My grandfather was, like the others, just as I remember him, though perhaps a little younger. His healthy, rosy appearance was probably due to him working outside in the air. I had known that between the wars he had worked on the estate, initially as a groundsman, as had his father before him. However, he also had a keen interest in horses and seemed to understand them. Because of this, he spent some of his time caring for the horses on the estate. His jolly and friendly character had made him a popular man.

"I'll put the kettle on, son. With Sister Mary on her way, she'll need plenty of hot water, I dare say." My father seems agitated and I watch him closely as he paces the floor.

"I know I've done it all before, but I still can't remember what I'm supposed to be doing, Pa."

"It's OK, the women will be fine. Just you stay here with me, my boy."

There is a knock at the door and my father hurries to open it. Standing there is a woman in uniform. I quickly ascertain that she is the midwife, Sister Mary. She is an attractive lady of about thirty years of age. Her manner is efficient as she quickly removes her dark coat, and matching hat, to display her pristine royal blue dress. She immediately begins to roll up her sleeves before donning a starched white apron and a set of cuffs. In her hand, she carries a large black bag. The tools of her trade, I assume.

"Thanks for coming so quickly, Sister," both men say simultaneously.

"That's OK, I was only helping out at the church hall. Mrs Coombes and her committee are trying to get ready for the arrival of another twelve evacuees from London, due to arrive on Wednesday. The nuns at the priory have agreed to take three from the same family. I don't know where we are going to put the others. I heard them mention your Dottie and Harry as possibly taking two of them. Poor things, having a bad time of it up there."

Sister Mary didn't wait for a reply as she focussed on the task in hand, "it's a bit early though, not due for another four weeks yet, probably a false alarm Daniel, and don't you go fretting yourself. I'll just pop up and see what's happening."

Leaving the kitchen, the midwife climbs the stairs calling up to her patient as she goes, "it's alright, my pet, I'm coming now."

I wait anxiously to see the outcome. My eyes are concentrated on the two men in front of me. My father looks worried. I watch him as he takes out a bottle of Dettol disinfectant from under the sink. His hands are shaking as he measures a cap full of the orange liquid and adds it to the tin bowl of hot water that Granddad is filling. In his hurry, he manages to spill a little of the liquid over Granddad's hand. I watch as the water turns a milky white and the smell of disinfectant fills the air.

"Pull yourself together, son or you won't be much good to Ruby when she needs you!"

I can hear low voices chattering, coming from upstairs, all sounding very calm. Then I hear footsteps descending the stairs; Sister Mary is smiling.

"Everything is OK. Ruby is in early labour, that's all. A long way to go yet. She's in good hands so I'm going to see another patient just down the lane, Mrs Jacob at number five. She had her baby yesterday and it won't feed. Just need to give the little one a talking to and then I'll be back. Shouldn't be more than half an hour. Have yourselves a cup of tea, it's going to be a long night! I just hope we are left alone tonight."

I am left feeling intrigued, as I don't know what she means by that last remark? She was putting on her hat and coat as she was talking, I had the impression that she was a bit of a chatterbox.

Shortly after she left, Nannie returned to the room.

"I think it would be a good idea to ask Dottie if she could collect the boys from school and keep them overnight. I know she won't mind."

I had forgotten that Auntie Dotty and Uncle Harry had lived next door. They never had any children of their own and I did not know why; however, they were very kind to my brothers and me. I hoped that I might have a glimpse of them.

My brothers and I had always been close. Douglas was the eldest, seven years older than me, and John was the middle child (two years younger than his brother). As a small child, I would tag along with them and join in with their games. Much of our play had been in the garden where we would build our dens. Sometimes we would play hide and seek in the apple orchard. When I was a little older, I was allowed to accompany them to the woods where I learnt to climb trees and play Cowboys and Indians. I didn't have any girl-friends until I started school!

There were times when I was not allowed to join the boys, specifically on the occasions when they were playing too far away from home, for my parents' comfort. There were also the male-only fishing excursions to the river, and times when they accompanied our granddad to the fields to catch rabbits. I am not sure if it's because I was a girl or if I had been too young to accompany them. On these occasions, I would entertain myself, playing with my toys. I had two dolls that I can remember fondly, one of which had been made by Auntie Dottie. Both she and Uncle Harry were quite talented when it came to needlework. I have memories of them sitting by the fireside in their cottage. Spread out on their laps would be a large piece of material and I would watch as they created beautiful embroidery using brightly coloured silks. It was years later when I learnt that my aunt had taught my uncle to sew.

Uncle Harry had been wounded in the Great War and his injuries had been quite severe. He always walked with a stick and his speech, I remember, was a little slurred. He had a small piece of skull-bone missing from his nearly bald head and where the skin had repaired itself, the wound had left an indentation. What had caused the wound, I did not know. I was fascinated by the movement within this indentation that seemed to pulsate and would try hard not to stare at my great uncle. I have no memories of the adults in my life ever talking about the Great War. I know it was not uncommon for wounded servicemen to learn some form of craft, as part of their occupational therapy. The nurse/patient friendship between these two had flourished; they fell in love and were later married.

My other free time was spent with Mum and Nannie; they had taught me the basic skills of sewing, knitting and cooking. Nannie would entertain me by turning wooden clothes pegs into little dolls. We would dress them in scraps of material and draw on their features.

I smile to myself as these memories of my early childhood return. I'd experienced a very happy childhood. At the age of seven though, things were about to change.

Together with my mother and two brothers, we moved into our own house. The cottage, like others on the estate, had been modernised to include an inside bath and toilet. Mum had a new job, working as a secretary in the estate offices and had been offered the cottage when the previous occupants had moved out. From a young child, through to adolescence, so would begin the next phase of my life.

Nannie gives the two men their instructions, then she ascends the stairs again to be with her daughter. The two men don their heavy coats, caps and scarves and leave by the back door. All is quiet. Across the room, I notice the sitting room door is slightly open. I have a desperate need to peer inside this room, to see if it's just as I remember.

The curtains were made from a heavy, green, brocade fabric. The suite consisted of an armchair, a second chair (without arms) and a chez-lounge completing the set. All had been of a similar fabric to the curtains. In the centre of the room had stood the oak dining-table and this was also covered with a paler green cloth. On those 'special' days, the table would be moved against the wall, to make space for the party games and dancing we all enjoyed.

Standing up from the window seat, I suddenly have an overwhelming feeling of dizziness and nausea and my head begins to throb once more. Concerned that I might throw up at any moment, I stagger towards the door. As I reach it, there is a mist forming around me that becomes increasingly dense as I cross the threshold into the adjoining room.

# Chapter 7

Blinking my eyes open, I realise that I am back in my own lounge and lying on the couch. I can hear the sound of a clock ticking. I am not alone for long as I can hear someone moving closer towards me. The fuzzy outline shape of a woman, but I cannot make out who it is.

"Mum, what are you doing? How did you manage to get down the stairs? You might have fallen! You promised you would ring the bell if you needed me, or Dad, for anything."

It's my daughter, Lottie, whose voice I can hear. There seems to be a 'mistiness' between us and things, and images are unclear. My stomach is churning and a vile bilious fluid fills my mouth. I begin to wretch and suddenly panic because I cannot find a suitable receptacle to vomit into. The heaving causes tremendous pain in my stomach and my back and I cry out for help. The contents of my stomach are expelled down the front of my clothes and onto the floor.

"It's OK, Mum, I'm here. Don't worry, I can clean it up."

I have a vile taste in my mouth. I dribble and then spit out more of the foul liquid. Unable to lift my pounding head, and feeling so weak, I lie motionless. Irritated voices are coming closer; someone is angry. It is a male voice.

"What are you doing leaving her, Lottie? How did she get down the stairs? She might have fallen!"

It is the voice of Jamie I can hear, but how can that be? I thought he was dead!

His angry voice reprimanding my daughter instantly brought me back to my senses. How dare he speak to Lottie like this! Overwhelmed with relief that I had just been dreaming, albeit a strange and surreal dream, I turn my thoughts to the defence of my daughter.

"It's not her fault, Jamie, for goodness sake, don't be angry with her. Be angry with me!"

A distraught Lottie cradles my head in her arms, and at the same time is apologising to her father, "I'm so sorry, Dad, I only popped out into the garden for a little while. The storm had blown open the gates and they were making a terrible noise. I was worried that it would disturb Mum. John was in the garden and saw me and he came across to ask after her. We were sheltering from the hail in the porch."

Kneeling down at my side, and through the haziness, I could now see Jamie's concerned face.

"It's OK, my love, I'm here. We're going to get you back upstairs to bed."

"Oh, please no, let me stay here in this room. It's where I want to be and I need to see my clock," I felt the tears coming again as I begged to be allowed to stay where I was.

"It's OK, Ann, calm down, we will sort something out, that's more comfortable for you. Mathew will be here later this evening and he can help bring the spare bed downstairs," Jamie stoops down and plants a kiss on my forehead. Feeling a little more in control, I smile at him and manage to lift my hand to fondly touch his cheek.

Lottie comes to my side and I can see that she now carries a bowl of water and that she has a towel over her shoulder.

"Mum, I'm going to give you a bit of a wash. That will help you feel better."

"Thank you, Nurse Lottie," I say with a smile, "I hope I'm not being too much of a burden to you?"

"Never a burden, Mum. I want to take care of you like you have always cared for me."

Every day I realised I was becoming a little weaker and as much as I tried to maintain my independency, I was finding it noticeably more difficult. When we had known that my illness was not going to improve, Lottie had insisted that she would share the responsibility of my care with her father. She was a gentle and thoughtful nurse and knew exactly how to guide me through my embarrassment of being cared for. Mothers instinctively notice changes in their children; in the last few days I have secretly suspected that Lottie may be pregnant, but I must wait patiently for confirmation of this. Time, however, may be running out for me.

The warm rose-scented water on my face and body helps to revive me a little. My nostrils are filled with the sweet smell of roses. If I close my eyes I can see clearly my grandmother's face, and she is smiling at me. Dressed in my clean night-shirt, I lie back on the pillows which support me and rest my aching body. I am weary and do not feel like making conversation. Bringing my daughter's hand to my lips, I kiss the hand of my angel.

"I love you so much, my darling. Never forget that."

We hold each other gently for a few moments. The pain is getting worse and I flinch.

"I'll give Jill a call. I think you may be ready for some more pain relief, Mum. She told me to call her anytime."

Agreeing with Lottie, I manage a little smile before I close my eyes, unable to bear the pain any more.

It is only when the morphine begins to wear off, that I become more rational in my thoughts. The pain is, daily, becoming more excruciating and I know that I am dying. My cancer has returned and this time, with a vengeance. My body is no longer able to fight off the disease that is spreading its torturous evil within me.

For the last five years, I have, overall, enjoyed a spell of reasonably good health. I would refer to this time as my second chance.

I was convinced that I had been one of the lucky ones because my cancer had been diagnosed early and the treatment had been successful. It felt strange that I should take ownership of the disease, always referring to it as 'my cancer'.

With every type of cancer, aggressive mutating cells affect individuals differently. Likewise, so the treatments do as well.

Therefore, I never took my second chance for granted. My life-style would have to change and I vowed to lead a healthier and stress-free life. I had persevered with my twice-weekly gym sessions and tried to follow a healthier diet. My late mother's words of wisdom reminded me to slow down, to try and enjoy the moment.

"Always take time to smell the roses," she would say.

On a few occasions, when I had felt particularly well and happy, I would overindulge and I still continued to enjoy a glass or two of wine.

Quite frankly, I had been devastated to learn that my cancer had returned. Feeling frustrated and angry, I was determined to fight for my life again. The oncology team had suggested a further course of treatment and I had agreed. They were not ready to give up on me and I resolutely would not let the big C get the better of me. After more sessions of chemotherapy, enduring once again the negative side effects, I would be told that sadly, this time the treatment had not worked. My body was beaten and my soul was despondent and I had to come to terms with the fact that I would eventually die.

In front of my family, I would appear strong. When I was left alone, I would cry pitifully to myself. In pain I would call out to God, challenging his power of healing, testing my own beliefs by begging for his help. There were times when I had even denied his existence.

"Why me," I would cry out; a bit silly really! After all, did I not know that I was not alone?

Statistically, one in three people are likely to have cancer sometime in their life. I am grateful, however, that Jamie was not one of them.

The dream I had experienced continued to puzzle me. Why had I seen so clearly, scenes from my past? What was the significance of the events leading up to my own birth?

The waves of pain rush over my body. I don't think I can wait much longer for my morphine.

# Chapter 8

All through my working life, I had been dedicated to my career in nursing. Entering the school of nursing at the age of eighteen meant that I knew little of life experiences. Training to be a nurse in the 1960s was so different from the way things are done now. The basis of teaching was far more practical and I believe now that this was for the better.

The first six weeks were spent in the school of nursing. The two rooms that made up the school of nursing were at the end of a long, winding, corridor. The only other room that utilised this area was the well-equipped library. I later learnt that the corridor had been added on to the hospital when it had been extended, to create two more wards and a new state of the art laboratory. High windows had been incorporated on the outside of the three rooms and this was the only source of natural light. Mostly, it was necessary to turn on the electric lights to ensure adequate visibility. The classroom was neatly spaced with twelve individual desks and chairs, just like any other school I had been into. The tutor's desk was at the front, facing the students. Next to this was a blackboard that stood on an easel and a full, life-size, skeleton that was named Mr Frame. The walls were covered with posters relating to health issues and physiological facts. That first morning in the school, we were asked to introduce ourselves to each other and talk a little about our reasons for wanting to become nurses. There were twelve students in total and for some reason, we were called 'set 10'. Among the students were five very young ladies from Malaysia.

With introductions over, we were marched out to the laundry rooms to collect our uniforms. We had been measured for these at an earlier date, once we had been accepted as suitable for the training. The royal blue, striped uniforms were highly starched, as were the aprons and caps. We each received a heavy navy blue out-door cape, lined in crimson red. Taken back into the classroom, we were shown how to fold our butterfly caps and indeed, how to attach them to our heads.

"Uniforms will be worn at all times. Aprons are only worn when working on the wards," Sister Jones, our tutor, had explained.

My first impression of this middle-aged lady, wearing a smart navy blue uniform and a frilly cap on her head, was that she was kind and quietly spoken, with a friendly face. For most of us this was the first time we had lived away from home and that, in itself, was a daunting prospect. Sister Jones was also the sister in charge of the nurses' home, where we would live, for the next three years. She was a kind and caring individual, who would continue to teach and nurture us as we developed the necessary skills to become qualified nurses.

My proud mother gave me a nurse's fob watch, which I wore then and continued to wear throughout my career.

The remainder of that first day was taken up by a tour of the wards, and various departments, that made up the hospital. Many times, in those first few days, I would take a wrong turn and get myself lost in the vast building of floors with its corridors winding in different directions. The hustle and bustle of movement and noise was intimidating!

The second day was the beginning of our learning and we went into the second of the two rooms which had been laid out like a nightingale ward, with three patients in a row. A female mannequin named Mrs Brown was tucked up in one of the beds. There was a gentleman in the second bed and a small child in a cot. During those first few weeks, the dummy patients would endure all manner of treatments, from basic hygiene to more invasive procedures, from a bedpan and bed bath to receiving injections and wound care. Roleplay was never one of my favourite ways to learn anything, but this we would have to do. Speaking out loud to the patients in these beds, and in front of colleagues and the nurse tutor, sometimes felt embarrassing. There were occasions when I, or a fellow student, would be reprimanded (by the tutor) for laughing if we had felt particularly amused at something that we were instructed to do or say.

Looking back, I believe that it had all been worthwhile for it gave us confidence in our ability to communicate with sick people and to show them how we cared. With the first eight weeks completed, and with a basic knowledge of anatomy and physiology, we were let loose on real patients. Moving in eight-week blocks from ward to ward, both medical and surgical, became the basis of our training. One day a week we would go back into school for theoretical learning and the opportunity to try out something else on poor Mrs Brown!

During my nursing training, I had spent a few weeks working alongside a community nurse. As much as I had enjoyed the experience, I decided that it wasn't for me and that I would prefer to care for patients in the hospital.

My friend Jill had completed her nurse training in one of the big London hospitals and had returned to her home county of Sussex afterwards, to find work. She had decided that London life was not for her. Our paths were to cross many times. She was of a similar age to me and had become a very knowledgeable and experienced nurse. Working as part of a palliative care team, she would look after patients within their own home environments whilst I would care for them in hospital. Some of her patients would need to spend some time in the hospital, for either surgical or medical treatments, and Jill would visit them often. Over the years, we had become close friends. With our respective partners also enjoying a friendship, we would socialise frequently. When our children were young, we had enjoyed many camping holidays together. We would often discuss our patients but only in the privacy of our homes and always with respect and dignity.

No one should under-estimate the importance of building both trust and confidentiality with someone suffering from cancer; those receiving treatments, or those who were terminally ill.

It was with Jill that I had been invited to attend a routine breast screening clinic. The mobile vehicle was parked in the hospital car park. I have seen some of these X-ray vehicles in supermarket car parks and thought this was a little strange. The screening is not a pleasant process but we both considered ourselves to be lucky to have the opportunity to have ourselves checked. There's no pain, just a little discomfort, and for some, maybe a little embarrassment. The radiographer has to place the breast onto a screening plate. A second plate is bought down and squashes the breast. Two X-rays are usually taken of each breast; one from above and one from the side. We were both lucky in the fact that we understood the process. Still, we are only human and being two girls together, we would often make light of it:

"I don't know how I'm going to fit my breast on the plate. I've not got much, never had," I had commented.

"And I'll have to help lift mine onto the plate as they are so heavy and have dropped to my waist," Jill replied.

"Oh the joys of middle age," I added with a giggle, "what with the night time sweats as well. I think I would like to come back as a man next time!"

How wonderful it was to have a friend that you could share your most intimate feelings with.

There would never be a day, following the screening, when I would not wonder how I would deal with cancer if I was to be told that I had this illness. Like so many other women, I would anxiously look through the post for the letter containing the results of my mammogram.

# Chapter 9

I can recall vividly the day that my test results finally came through and when my life would change forever.

Working fulltime, and shift work, usually meant that I would have two days off each week. If, however, I had been working night shifts, I would enjoy a longer period of time off. I'd always spend my first non-working day catching up with mundane chores and, if time would allow, enjoy one of my favourite pastimes, like baking. Jamie and the children were critics of my culinary 'talent' and I was rewarded, mostly, with positive comments. My second day, I would keep for spending time with family and friends.

It was on this particular day, with hands that had been covered in flour up to my elbows when the phone had rung.

The caller had been a nurse, informing me of a concern that they had with my mammogram results. She had been quick to add that it was probably nothing but that they would like me to have an ultrasound scan.

As hard as I tried, I could not respond. My mouth was dry and a response failed me. Silence at the other end of the line provoked a necessary reassurance from the caller.

"At this stage, it is just routine procedure. Sometimes mammogram results are inconclusive and we just want to double-check. Can you hear me, Ann?"

"Yes, sorry. I'm just trying to take it all in."

"That's OK, I quite understand. Is there anything else you would like to ask me?"

I had many questions but knew they probably wouldn't be cohesive at this time as my brain was in a state of utter confusion, too in shock to take in information just now. "Perhaps I had better wait for the scan results."

After Jamie, Jill was the first person I had called. I was a complete and utter wreck. Within the hour, she was by my side, not just the caring nurse but my friend. She would be there throughout my treatment supporting not only me but a confused and frightened Jamie too. She was there, sharing in the turbulent months that followed. The best friend anyone could have wished for.

The clock chimed, telling me it was five o'clock and it was now quite dark outside. The storm had come and gone. The weather continued to be mild for the time of year. The whole country was experiencing unusual weather for the season. I had not been out of the house for at least a week and the days preceding this, I only left to wander in the garden, in between showers, to take exercise and check that all was well. I had been amazed to see a few roses still in bloom. There were also daffodil buds waiting to burst open. What a strange December this was turning out to be.

A knock at the door, followed soon after by the sound of a cheery voice, disturbed my thoughts. Jamie reached the door as Jill came in. Under her coat, she would be wearing her uniform, as she was on duty and visiting me as one of her patients.

"Hi, Jamie, how is my favourite patient today?" She mostly spoke out loud enough for me to hear. Right from the beginning, I had insisted that there would not be any whispering in the corners about me, whether out of kindness or concern.

"Been a bit naughty today, Nurse Jill," came the cheeky response.

Being in so much pain, I allowed my feelings of resentment, towards Jamie's statement, to wash over me. All I wanted was for the formalities to conclude quickly so that Jill could get on with administering my medication.

"Hello, Ann, how are you feeling this evening? Jamie tells me you managed to get down the stairs by yourself, you naughty girl."

She always greeted me with a gentle hug.

"A little better, thanks," I lied.

Why would I say this? How can I feel a little better when I know full well that I am in so much pain, that I am dying!

"The pain is getting worse, Jill. I think I could do with some more pain relief now."

"Let me just check your temperature and have a listen in." Placing a thermometer under my tongue, she put the earpieces of the stethoscope into her ears and continued with her observations. "OK, you're running a bit of a temperature, not unexpected though. How are you coping with the morphine?"

Remembering poor Lottie, who had to clean up after me earlier, reminded me to tell Jill about this other new problem.

"It certainly helps with the pain but I do feel a little nauseous at times."

Turning to her bag, she brought out two glass ampoules of drugs. "Doctor Thorn has suggested that we increase your pain relief, and he has prescribed something to help with the nausea if you need it. But you must promise not to go up and down the stairs on your own - promise!"

I knew that the morphine increase was heading for the maximum dose that I could have. The next step would be a continuous intravenous infusion and possible transfer to the local hospice as an inpatient. If I have any say in this matter it will not happen, and I can be very stubborn when I want to be.

"Not going to be a problem, Jill. Mathew will be here soon. He's coming home for Christmas, early. He has some leave due, so will be having an extended holiday."

Inwardly, I believe that this has all been prearranged; because my condition is deteriorating fast.

"He and Jamie are going to bring a bed downstairs for me. I much prefer to be in this room. I can keep an eye on everyone," I added with a smile.

The drugs quickly start to take effect and the pain is deadening; reduced to a feeling of a dull, gnawing, sensation.

"That's great, Ann. Now, remember you can call me anytime. I mean that, day or night. You're not just my patient but my dearest friend."

She quickly looked away and I thought I noticed her wiping away a tear. Always maintaining her professional position, she checked I was still managing to eat a little food and then whispered in my ear, "Have you managed a poo yet?"

"No, I haven't, not for a couple of days now. I am eating a little of Pete's soup and fruit puree, he is making for me though. I'm sure it will help."

Pete was continually trying to tempt me with small tasty meals that he prepared daily in his kitchen. This was his way of helping me and supporting his wife, Lottie.

"I am quite spoilt," I assured her.

"And so you should be. Is there anything else I can do for you, Ann?"

"No, I don't think so, thank you, Jill. Jamie can help me get to the bathroom later for a wash."

I always tried to wait until I needed the toilet more urgently, before making the difficult and painful journey to the bathroom.

"Giving me a farewell hug then," she whispered in my ear. "Love you lots, I'll see you tomorrow."

"Thank you, Jill. Love you too. Now get off home to your family, it's getting late."

Pulling the door closed behind her, as she left, meant that I couldn't clearly hear the conversation between herself and Jamie, as they met in the hallway. I called out to them both:

"Are you two whispering about me?"

Jamie had opened the door to the porch and I could feel a slight draft. I could make out discrete voices in conversation.

Jill retreated back to the hallway and poked her head around the lounge door. She was smiling as she teased me, "Just discussing, giving you an enema tomorrow!"

"Don't think so. Not as bad as that yet," I replied quickly, smiling back at her.

The injection of morphine, which had now taken full effect, gave me the courage to enjoy her banter. The pain was easing and I felt better about myself.

Only with determination would I manage to stay awake to see Mathew, before the drug-induced sleep would take hold.

Due to the bad weather, earlier that afternoon, Mathew arrived home later than was expected. Everyone had been feeling a little apprehensive until the sound of his car could be heard pulling up the drive. Greetings were completed only after I had thrown my arms around his neck and planted little kisses all over his face, moistened by my tears and telling him how happy I was to have him home at last.

Lottie came out of the kitchen when she heard his voice and ran into his arms.

"It's so lovely to see you, Matt. Now we can all be together for Christmas, just like last year."

Lottie and Mathew were always close, ever since they had grown up. This, I remembered, had not always been the case when they were younger. Typical sibling rivalry, where Jamie and I tried hard not to take sides for fear of making things even more volatile between them.

"You two will just have to sort it out between you. Stop and listen to each other and work it out," Jamie would suggest.

This had obviously worked, for both children had grown closer to each other in their teens. Mathew would then always look out for Lottie whenever he felt she needed intervention from an older brother.

"I know you have just arrived, mate," stated his father, "but I need your help to bring a bed down for Mum. She wants to sleep downstairs, so she can keep an eye on us."

It was lovely to hear everyone laughing. In a short time, a bed was easily carried down the stairs for me. Lottie made it up and brought down my favourite over-blanket; the soft, woollen, tartan blanket that had been a gift from Lottie and Pete last Christmas, and I loved it.

"Sorry to be such a nuisance but I know I shall be much happier here in the lounge."

"Don't ever think you are being a nuisance, Mum," scolded Lottie, smiling. "Anyway, we all know that you don't want to miss anything," she added teasingly.

Feelings of contentment washed over me as I observed my family, all together. I had to be content with listening, rather than partaking in conversation, due to the increasing feeling of drowsiness. It was cosy in the dimmed light, and the warm fire, as we spent time catching up with each other's news.

A light supper was prepared by Jamie and enjoyed on trays in the cosiness of the lounge. All good things must come to an end. I stifled a yawn and my family appreciated my tiredness and as night began to draw to a close, each made their own excuse to bid me goodnight.

A kiss and a hug followed by, "good night and God bless you," to each one, ended a lovely evening. Jamie, however, would stay a little longer.

"I don't really like you being alone down here and I certainly will miss the cuddles in our bed. I think, on second thoughts, I might sleep on the couch next to you."

"No, that will not be necessary," I assured him that I was quite happy to be left on my own to sleep downstairs.

Jamie assisted me in getting to the bathroom on the ground floor, which up until now had been infrequently used; with my teeth cleaned, I tried again (unsuccessfully) to do a poo and wondered if Jill had been serious about my need for an enema? Inwardly, I was concerned that my internal organs were beginning to fail me.

With his arm supporting me, Jamie helped me back to bed. The door to his study had been opened and I could see the wheelchair placed ready for when I would no longer have the strength to walk. I shook my head in despair as I had already told Jill that I would not need it. Somehow they had managed to smuggle it in without my knowledge.

"It's only there in case you need it." Jamie could obviously see from my expression, that I was annoyed at their defiance.

Fussing around me for a while, ensuring that I had everything I needed, including a call bell, I was eventually left for the night. I listened as, upstairs, Jamie got himself ready for bed and then all was quiet in the house. All alone now, I could quietly whisper my prayers and allow myself to shed a few tears of self-pity. I decided that I would take an extra morphine tablet, just to see me through to the morning.

Mesmerised by the subtle sound of the ticking clock, my body started to relax. Experiencing an unusual sense of well-being, I close my eyes and begin to drift slowly into a state of unconsciousness. My mind was now in a state of euphoria; I felt happiness, and I did not understand why.

Opening my eyes, the room appears to be surrounded in a bright light. Surely it could not be daylight yet. I try to keep them closed but cannot do so. Unlike daylight, it is now almost neon in appearance and I cannot take my eyes from it. My body responds, as I easily pull myself to a sitting position. The enticing light has movement in it as if it is dancing in front of me. Now, raised to a standing position, I cannot feel anything solid beneath my feet. Suspended in the air, I begin to float forward always following the light. Everything is beautiful and I feel so happy. Stepping through, into the intensity of the brightness, I am surrounded by the light. There's nothing solid, above or below me.

Slowly, the light begins to fade and darkness returns. I find myself, once again, back in the kitchen of my grandparents' house. The room is almost in darkness; all except for the dimmest light of an oil lamp which stands on the dresser. There is a small fire in the hearth; its embers glowing red and orange, showing signs of extinguishing. From upstairs, the muffled sounds of voices and whimpering can be heard. Wondering where everyone could be, I walk across to the other side of the room. Who would leave an unattended fire or a lit oil lamp, I muse? Perhaps they have all gone upstairs to bed? With anticipated eagerness, I wait to see once again who will come down the stairs to turn off the lamp and allow me more visions from my past?

# Chapter 10

A droning noise, coming from outside the house, steals my attention and I am inquisitive to see what it is. Moving to the cosy window seat and then lifting a corner of the heavy black-draped curtains, I peek out. In the distance, and high in the sky, small planes are approaching flying in formation across the night sky. The roaring sounds of the engines are getting louder as they get closer. From somewhere on the ground, beams of light are projected into the night sky and the sound of heavy, booming, gunfire intermingles with the noise of the engines. An explosive mixture of sparks lights up the night sky, identifying the individual planes. Smaller planes are approaching from another direction and the sound of rapid firing can be heard. A dogfight begins, the planes begin rolling, diving and climbing again. Trails of smoke, interspersed with flashes of fire, light up the skies.

The deafening sound of a plane falling to earth, twisting as it does so, is followed by an explosion, which causes the house to shake. From the second floor comes the sound of a woman's scream and a baby's cries, as if taking its first breath.

The dogfight is over. The guns are silenced. Some of the planes appear to group together again and continue on to their destination, while others appear to scatter in all directions. I would not know whether the enemy planes were on a bombing raid to London, and had been intercepted or if they were returning, having successfully completed their mission to once again cause devastation to our beautiful historic city and its vulnerable, exhausted, brave citizens. How surreal it was, to experience an event like this!

Up until now, I could only have imagined the harrowing effect that something like this must have had on families, and communities, during the time of war. I can remember my mother saying to me that she hoped that I would never have to experience living through a war. My only insight into factual knowledge, about Britain at war, had been through watching old newsreels and reading books on the subject.

Both of my brothers have a few memories of their life during this period but time has almost erased the pinnacle points that the young boys would have likely shared with their friends whilst playing at games of war pretending to be British pilots, with their arms outstretched, flying in the skies and fighting off the enemy (or dropping their bombs). Maybe they would have made guns from sticks, found in the woods, and held battles with their imaginary enemies?

There is a sudden rattle of metal against wood; someone is eagerly trying to enter from outside the house. As the door opens, my grandfather stumbles as he trips over the threshold in his haste to get in. His dishevelled and grubby appearance is evidence of what had just taken place outside. Removing his tin hat and heavy overcoat, which he drops to the floor, and with his boots still on, he rushes to the stairs but is stopped in his tracks by Nannie. She has only now reached the bottom of the stairs and even in the dim light, her blood-stained clothes and staining to her arms and face, are conspicuous enough for me to know that all was not well upstairs. In a distraught, frantic, manner she almost collapses into the arms of my grandfather.

I want so much to help them but I seem to be pinned down to my seat. With my ghostly arms, I reach out to them but cannot feel anything solid to touch. Of course, I remind myself that I am dreaming. These distressing events, no matter how real they seem, were just figments of my imagination. I will wake up soon and this will become just a memory, a memory which will fade, just as dreams do.

"It's alright, Megan, I'm here now. It was a close one, I must say. The Williams's house has taken a direct hit."

Interrupting and almost begging to be heard, Nannie looked up to my grandfather's face.

"You don't understand; I didn't mean for it to happen. I had to do it. There was no other choice."

Taking her by the shoulders, my grandfather gently shakes her.

"Calm down, Megan and tell me what has happened."

"It's the baby; Ruby has had the baby, but there was a second one."

"Twins," he shouts, "but that's…"

Before he can say anything else, he is interrupted again. "No, it's not. If only we had been better prepared. This bloody war! If only Sister Mary could have been with us, she would have known what to do."

Grabbing my grandfather by the hand, she leads him up the stairs, wearing his muddy boots, and I am left to speculate as to what had occurred upstairs that was causing so much distress to my family.

Someone is shouting outside the house. I cannot make out what is being said. Then I hear someone calling, distinctively, for help. Seconds later, a commotion has erupted. If anyone was hoping to sleep tonight they were (I thought to myself) going to be disappointed. Voices were now mingling with the sound of sirens which leads me to believe that the situation, for now, is over but I suspect there is devastation outside these walls, as well as inside.

Within a few minutes, my grandparents have returned to the kitchen. The expressions on their faces were enough to tell me that something tragic had happened upstairs. Nannie reached for paper and pen while Granddad poked the fire and took coal from the scuttle to add to the dying embers.

"Take this note to Reverent Coombes, he will know what to do and tell Sister Mary that Ruby has had her baby, and to come as soon as she can."

"Do you want me to find Daniel and send him home too?"

"No, let him finish his job first. From what I heard, and what you have been telling me, I dare say there is more to do out there than he can do in here."

"I'll check on Dotty and the boys too. I know they got to the garden shelter in time."

Walking up to Nannie, I watched as a gentle, loving man tilted the blood and tear-stained face of a very sad lady and planted a soft, reassuring, kiss upon her lips.

"Try not to worry, my dear. You did your best, as you always do and God, who sees all, will be forgiving."

My grandfather retrieved his coat, which was laid on the floor, and put it back on. He took a scarf, which was hung on a peg, nailed to the back door, and tied it around his neck.

Pulling up his collar, he went out into the darkness of the night.

I was puzzled as to what could have occurred in the house, which could possibly require the services of a clergyman?

Nannie stoked the fire and she also added more fuel. I watched her as she sat down in Granddad's chair. Her expression was one of pitiful sadness and I looked on helplessly as she took out a handkerchief from the pocket of her apron to wipe away the tears that were now beginning to flow. Folding her arms in front of her, she began rocking backwards and forwards as tears rolled down her pale cheeks; crying softly to herself, so no one else in the house would hear her.

A weak call, from a woman upstairs, and Nannie abruptly ceases her crying and pulls herself together. Blowing her nose and wiping her face for one last time, she makes her way to the stairs, calling up to the woman with confidence as she disappears from my sight.

"It's alright, my pet, I'm coming now."

I recall the words of endearment 'my pet'. As a child, she would often use them when referring to me.

"How I love you, Nannie," I whisper.

It only seems a few minutes before she returns to the kitchen again. As she enters the room, she is carrying a small bundle. Her eyes are filling with more tears as she holds the object close to her. Walking across the room and closer to the now fiercely burning fire, I observe as she lifts the bundle to her face and plants a kiss upon it.

Someone taps the door softly and she moves across the room to answer it. She fumbles as she lifts the heavy latch, protective of the small linen package that she holds. The door is then opened, revealing the visitor. A very tall man, wearing a long black coat and a large-brimmed hat, is standing in the aperture of the door. He makes no intention of entering. I cannot make out his features as they are obscured by a scarf that is wrapped around his face. The swaddling bundle is handed to him. He bows his head as he takes it from my grandmother's arms. No words are exchanged. With his free hand, he gently touches my grandmother on her shoulder. Turning away, he walks into the first signs of an early dawn and a new day.

From upstairs my mother cries out in anguish and it is echoed with the sound of a newborn baby's cry. My grandmother returns upstairs to comfort her daughter. The room is quiet except for the sound of the fire, as it crackles with a new life.

Feeling a hint of deep sadness, I bring my hands up to cover my face. I am filled with an overwhelming sense of grief, but I cannot fully understand the reason why.

The clock strikes midnight and there are enough chimes to awaken me from my unconscious state. Feelings of anger come over me at the untimely intrusion into my dreams. I thought I was being given a second glimpse into my past. Events that had occurred, which had led up to the time of my birth which I knew, seemingly, to be correct from my mother's own account. Restless, but not from pain, my subconscious state of mind works hard to fathom out the meaning of it all. Everything had seemed so real and factual, and yet I realise it must have only been a dream. Perhaps if I can fall asleep again, I will be able to understand more?

Obviously, this is not to be. Awake now and not wanting to disturb anyone else's sleep, I turn on the night light that sits on the table next to me. The African animal characters, which are moulded to its base, light up. It had been a gift from my mother to Mathew when he had been born and as he grew, he had become very fond of it. We had also used it for Lottie. As infants, they had both been afraid to go to sleep in the dark and the light it produced was subtle enough to help them overcome this problem.

The irony was that I could never sleep with a light on. Picking up a pen and notebook, that I kept by my side, I proceed to jot down aspects of my dreams. By doing this, I had hoped to be able to rationalise their meanings. It's not long before I have written down all that I could remember.

The simplest of things tire me out. From upstairs I could hear that someone was moving about and then I knew that Jamie was coming down the stairs. Perhaps I had not been as quiet as I had previously thought.

"Sorry, Jamie, hope I didn't wake you? I am trying to be quiet."

"I heard sounds and then noticed you had turned on the light, so knew that you must be awake. I thought you might like a bit of company."

Smiling, he came towards me and I shuffled to make room for him on my bed. Together, we lay closely, as it was only a single bed. Jamie supported my head on his arm as we clung together.

"Sorry it's a bit cramped," I added.

"Cosy," came the reply.

Never, in all our years of marriage, had I been given any cause to doubt Jamie's love for me and equally mine for him. Like most couples, we had our ups and downs, and disagreements. My illness had put a different perspective on our relationship now. Every moment we now shared had become special. We were both prepared for the outcome we knew was inevitable and that I now believed was fast approaching.

"Jamie, can I tell you about my dreams? They are so vivid and I am so confused."

"Come on then, love, tell me a story."

He smiled because I had always told him about the dreams that had seemed so real to me. Those, in particular, that had caused me anxiety. "But remember, my love, what Jill had told us. Some of the side effects of taking morphine can cause confusion and hallucinations."

"Yes, I know that but I cannot help wondering why the details in my dreams are so vivid."

Side by side and feeling relaxed, I relayed to him my curious dreams. To start with, he found some aspects amusing, especially the cow in the kitchen. Not once, however, did he try to interrupt me. He listened intensely and seemed especially interested when I told him about the wartime air raid that had occurred at the same time as I was being born. This he had found particularly intriguing. When I had finished, he tried to rationalise all that I had told him.

Unlike me, Jamie never believed in ghosts or anything supernatural. As far as he was concerned, there had to be a logical explanation for everything. For a few minutes, we lay quietly, enjoying the close proximity. I could not read his mind but thought that he would dismiss what I had told him and say no more, so I was quite astonished when he continued the conversation, still showing an interest in what I had just divulged to him.

"Any chance you were one of the twins? Strange things happened in the war; it was a difficult time for everyone. Can you imagine what it must have been like giving birth in the middle of the night, with a dog fight going on?"

"Yes, I know. Mum told me the story over and over again."

I had loved my mother so much and missed her greatly when she had died. There had been many times when she would remind me of how lucky I had been, the night I had been born, but would always say how grateful she was that we would never experience the horrors of war.

"I think I would have known if I had been a twin, wouldn't I?"

"I guess so, but even I am finding some aspects of your dreams curious."

How reassuring it was to have Jamie share my concerns.

"Time to rest now, my love. Tomorrow, I will do some research and see if we can find out more. I love you always."

"I love you always too. God bless."

Within minutes, it seems, he was asleep beside me. I listened to his soft breathing and pulled the blanket over his shoulder, lest he should feel the cold.

The pain was returning but I did not want to disturb my husband, sleeping beside me. Lying next to him, I tried to breathe through the pain and my thoughts went to my mother and her labour pains. It must have been a terrible ordeal, for any woman, to go through labour during the war; not knowing when the next air raid would come. I thought of the many women that had been left coping alone, while their husbands were away fighting for our country. How many grandparents had taken on the support role for the families and just like my grandmother had not only helped with bringing up their grandchildren but had been present at the birth of the new babies as well?

Repeating my grandmother's words to my father, I whispered to myself, "Babies will come when they are ready." Giving birth to my two children had been well managed and uneventful. I have been very lucky in that respect. "God bless you both," I whispered again to myself.

My body and my mind feel so tired. The pain within me is fighting to keep me from sleep. How long will I have before I close my eyes for the last time? There are times now when the pain is too much to bear, and I am left clinging to life by a thread.

Closing my eyes, I can visualise a woman who I believe is my mother. She is standing close in front of me and if I reach out, I think I can touch her. She is much younger than I remember. In her arms, she is holding a baby who is sleeping peacefully and she pulls back the shawl covering its face. I can see its small delicate features. My mother smiles at me and then blows me a kiss.

Behind my mother, I can see a bright light and watch as it grows dimmer. My mother seems to be drawing back towards it. I don't want her to go. "Please don't leave me," I plead, "can't I come with you?"

"Not yet, Rosemary, it's not your time. Have patience, my love and be brave. We will soon be together, I promise."

She is gone and I feel bereft.

# Chapter 11

The birds are confused in the wake of the changing weather and I am woken by their beautiful sound bringing with it the promise of a new dawn. Yesterday's storm has passed. The skies are clear and blue, with fast-moving puffs of white cloud that play hide and seek with the sun. The trees are almost bare of their leaves, exposing branches that continue to sway in the more gentle winds. The sun is giving out a tantalising spectrum of coloured light, which shines through the gaps at the windows where the curtains do not quite meet. The crystal pendants are motionless as they dangle from their threads, between the folds of fabric, but they still emit their rainbow patterns around the room. It is so beautiful and I want it to last forever.

I take a few precious moments to gather my thoughts, to recollect the strange things that have happened to me in the days and nights preceding this one. I am not sure how much can possibly be factual and how much is down to my state of mind. I can graphically describe things that I have seen that, as far as I know, I can have no knowledge of.

For the last few days, when I have awoken from my sleep, I have fought strong feelings of agitation and confusion. Although the weird dreams of the night before will undoubtedly continue to haunt me, I am determined this morning to be more like Jamie and try to rationalise their meanings. I know that the increasing amount of morphine, which is being injected into my body, is probably the underlying cause of such fantastic dreams. Therefore, with those thoughts clearer in my head, I close my eyes - and in silence, I pray.

I thank God for giving me another day. I pray for forgiveness for having doubt in his love for me and ask that when death finally comes, I will be strong in mind and ready in my soul and that I may be accepted into heaven. Always I pray for Jamie, who is my rock. Without him, I know I could not have coped.

He has been there from the beginning; was by my side when I awoke, following surgery, and cared for me while I underwent both chemotherapy and radiotherapy. The gruelling process that I thought would lead me to recovery, had been arduous. We had made that journey together. The cancer had gone, or so we thought, and our love for each other remained strong. In time, the physical side to our relationship had returned and for a short time, I had almost felt whole again.

My prayers included the children.

It has not been an easy task, coming to terms with the certainty of premature death; however, I have tried to support my family by remaining strong in their presence. Reassuring them that I am not afraid of dying and that they must accept the things that cannot be changed and move forward.

I remember the words of Jamie's favourite prayer: The Serenity Prayer. There have been numerous occasions when he has spoken the words out loud to one of us, reminding us of the important things in life. Indeed, I remember occasions when the table was turned and either myself, Mathew or Lottie have reminded him of the same meaningful words of the prayer:

"God grant me the serenity to accept the things I cannot change, the courage to change the things I can and wisdom to know the difference."

The children have heard the prayer spoken so many times that they too can recite the words easily. Sighing softly to myself, as I recall some of those incidences, brings a smile to my face; how lucky I am having such a wonderful family around me.

In my prayers, I remember those that are lonely, especially the elderly and the sick.

It doesn't seem that long ago when I had lost my faith in God, completely blaming him for the unfairness of my illness. When a close and dear friend of ours had been diagnosed with bowel cancer, and following treatment was subsequently cured, I became angry at the injustice.

What had I done to deserve this? Why did he not die? Why do I have to die? Why is there no cure for me? After all, had I not tried to be a good person?

As a child, I had been brought up in a Christian community. I had enjoyed attending Sunday school with my big brothers and had accompanied the adults to church services. I had been encouraged to say my prayers before going to sleep at night. Not such a goody-goody when I look back to my teenage years though there were times when I would rather spend my weekends with my friends, especially those of the opposite sex. Indeed, I can think of one particular occasion when I had rowed with my mother because I did not want to go to church one Sunday morning, because some of my friends were going to a pop concert and I had wanted to go too.

Challenging my mum wasn't easy.

"You don't have to go to church every Sunday. I'm sure God won't mind if I miss the odd one now and again."

"I always look forward to you accompanying me to church, Rosemary," she had said, "and the service only lasts for an hour."

"That's not the point," I continued to argue, "all of my friends are going early so that they can be as close to the stage as possible."

I never thought that I needed to go to church every week to be a good Christian, and I knew a lot of my friends had felt the same way. On this occasion, my mother relented and even though she said that she would be disappointed, when I got home that evening, it was to find that she had spent the day with a male friend that she had apparently met in church. After this, it became easier to skip the odd Sunday tradition of attending the morning service.

There were times, when I was in my late teens and early twenties, that I would be away from home and during this time, there would be long periods when I did not go to church. Things changed again when I became a parent myself. I was determined to see that my children were baptised and taken to church. Both Jamie and I agreed that we would encourage them to attend but that when they were old enough, they could make up their own minds.

And so it was that Mathew and Lottie, from a young age, were taken to Sunday School where I would sometimes participate in teaching the lessons. As teenagers, they participated in the service and had also enjoyed the church youth club. I had encouraged Jamie to help out with organising appropriate games and outings for the youth of our village.

Sundays were always kept as a special day and, following the morning service, I would go home and prepare a delicious Sunday roast. This was always a favourite with everyone.

I've always tried to help those in need and donated to charities, especially during times of world famine and natural disasters. As a family, we would watch television relief programmes. Like thousands of people all over the country, I would cry when watching the desperation of individuals caught up in such scenarios. Those trying desperately to find lost family or just wanting to live a peaceful life, rearing their families in a safe environment. I did not, however, blame God for the catastrophic world tragedies of war and famine but instead, would accuse world leaders and governments of not doing enough to prevent them from happening in the first place.

Remembering the many friends and family that I have loved and lost, together with those still with me, had finally helped me to come to terms with my cancer, even knowing that it would eventually take my life. It was not just family and friends, the daily news often reported on celebrity deaths and some of these too had been from cancer. They were not all strangers to me though as they habitually come into my lounge, to entertain me through radio and television. I had become quite fond of some of them.

My re-evaluation from doubting in my own beliefs in God became absolute at Easter of this past year. I had been attending a gym session on the morning of Good Friday. As I peddled away on the static bicycle, training machine, or briskly walked on the treadmill, I connected my earpiece to the television controls.

This, I had done on each occasion on which I had attended the gym in the past, as it was always an opportunity to catch up on the day's news and current events. The morning programmes also offered a selection of topical issues and would have the occasional guest or celebrity chef, who would do a step by step guide on how to produce a delicious meal in easy stages. I particularly enjoyed those.

However, on this occasion, being a religious day, there had been a documentary looking at the part played by Judas Iscariot in the story of Easter. He was the disciple that had apparently betrayed Jesus for thirty pieces of silver. The story, I had remembered well, was now being questioned by the presenter of the programme. Whatever his motive was, no one can know for certain. The scenarios that were presented would go on to leave doubt in my own mind. Following the crucifixion of Christ, Judas had taken his own life. The listeners were being left, by the presenter, to ponder on the importance of forgiveness. Did Judas know that he would have been forgiven, before taking his life?

In all honesty, I think there is a little of Judas in me. The stories of Christ tell me that he forgave all those who truly repent. If I believe in him then I must know for certain that I have been forgiven for my sins. These thoughts would help to ease my life's deep regrets.

I remind myself that death is a sure outcome for everyone at some time and in a moment of quiet, I reflect.

"If my time is soon, then so be it. I will not be frightened."

It is with my conscience clearer and with continued prayer that I feel more at ease with myself and can prepare for death.

Overall, I feel the pain is getting worse, or maybe my tolerance is simply lessening. There are good days and bad days. On a good day, like today, I feel grateful to be alive. On a bad day, when the pain becomes intolerable, I find myself inwardly crying out for the end to come.

Because I did not need to top up on my morphine overnight, this morning my mind was a little clearer. The pain was still present but not gnawing at my insides as it had been the day previous to this one. However, the ache in my bones continually and progressively gets worse on a daily basis. I find it is getting increasingly difficult and painful to move. The nurse in me knows that cancer pain can vary from patient to patient. Individuals have different pain thresholds and with some cancers, people can experience little or no pain at all.

Jamie lies still next to me but stirs as I try to move to make myself more comfortable. Taking a deeper breath and through gritted teeth, I manage to draw my knees up ever so slightly. Slowly it is then possible to turn onto my side. He is a light sleeper and I see that I have woken him.

"Morning, my love," I greet him with a forced smile.

Jamie turned over to face me so that we were lying side by side.

"You're right," he exclaimed, "this bed is a bit too small for the both of us. I hope I haven't disturbed you too much?"

Not wanting to cause him additional concern, I answer positively, telling him a white lie, "I had quite a good sleep, thank you."

Jamie yawns noisily and I have to remind him not to wake the children.

The clock chimes for six-thirty.

"It's still early, Jamie and the kids deserve to sleep in. Why don't you go back upstairs and get some more sleep yourself?"

"You know me, when I'm awake, I can't go back to sleep," he replied. "Anyway, I have lots to do today and I have a job I want to complete before Christmas. I can't believe it's the seventeenth already! And that reminds me, it's your birthday tomorrow."

I had completely forgotten about my birthday.

"Yes, I guess it must be," I replied.

Being able to enjoy one last Christmas was more important to me than celebrating another birthday. It's quite an insignificant celebration when you know that you are dying. After all, it doesn't matter anymore that I will be another year older. I am hanging on and hoping that I will spend one more Christmas with my family.

Feeling sorrowful again, I recall that last conversation I had had with my doctor. The results from blood tests, following a routine check-up, had come back. The cancer would not be beaten. I was filled with such a range of emotions; anger, denial and disappointment. After all, other than a general feeling of tiredness, I had not experienced any other symptoms.

Doctor Thorn had been the family GP for a number of years and we knew each other well. I had rarely needed to seek medical advice personally and had considered myself to be fit and healthy, most of the time. My visits to the surgery had mainly been to take one or other of my children when I had thought that they should be seen by a doctor. However, we did also meet at times when he would visit the hospital to see one of his patients. We had also met at occasional meetings and lectures.

Sitting in his surgery, on this particular occasion, he had found it quite difficult talking to me about my prognosis. An expert in his field of general practise, he was also an expert in oncology. It was probable that because we had known each other professionally, that was why he had seemed to find it so difficult to talk to me.

I had insisted that he tell me how long I had left to live. He appeared to fumble with his words. Perhaps he wasn't used to his patients being so blunt, but I needed to know.

"You are asking me a very difficult question. My answer will be broad because, in all honesty, I do not know."

"I appreciate that, but I need to have some idea as to how long I will have? For example, how much time am I likely to spend feeling as well as I do now before I start to become unwell?"

"You might have a few months, you could even have a year and maybe you will have more."

I was baffled and angered by his staggered reply, "Will I live to see another Christmas?" I asked, thinking to myself how it was only March.

Peering at me over the top of his spectacles, he went quiet. I could see that he was struggling to find the right words.

"I cannot say exactly, Ann, how long it will be. I don't want to give you false hope but then again, I don't want to be too pessimistic. Just know that we will all do our very best for you. I wish I could offer you more hope, but in all honesty, I cannot."

At last, he was being more forthright.

"I need to make arrangements. I have so much to do. I don't want to leave things for Jamie and the children to sort."

Realising I was babbling on, Doctor Thorn got up from his chair and came out from behind his desk. Pulling up a chair close to me, he sat down and took my hands in his.

"I will always be here for you, Ann, you can count on that and you know how it all works, having worked in palliative care yourself."

I suppose it does help to have an insight into the care that would be made available to me.

"That takes care of the day to day needs then."

My reply caused the doctor to raise his eyebrows. He had probably expected me to burst into tears.

"I am hurting and very angry," I told him. "I don't mean to appear ungrateful but I don't know how to deal with these feelings."

Doctor Thorn had been regularly attending the same church as I did. Knowing, therefore, that religion played an important part in my life, it was his suggestion that I should talk to our local vicar.

With the weekend off, I decided to attend the Sunday morning communion service. Accompanied by Jamie and Lottie, we had sat in our usual pew. On occasions, when this pew was already taken, we would happily sit in another but I was pleased to find our familiar pew available.

Two rows in front of me I could see Dr Thorn sitting with his wife. Whenever I had seen them together, I thought that they had made the perfect couple. On this Sunday, I wondered how long it would be before our doctor would retire. How lucky they were to still enjoy good health as they both reached their senior years.

Throughout the service, I had failed to concentrate on the lessons and the sermon. If I had to answer questions on what the vicar had said, I would have had no idea. When it was time to stand and read aloud the creed, the words poured out of my mouth and yet all the time I was thinking about my anger. During the quiet time as we knelt for prayers, I had once again not heard the words spoken, or responded, as I usually had except when a prayer was read for those who had passed away. Now as I listened, I wanted to understand the necessity to pray for those who have recently departed from this world.

If, as I was led to believe, all sins are forgiven then what was the reason for praying for those who had already died?

As we stood to sing the hymns, I found that my mouth was dry and it was difficult to sing. Glancing up I had noticed Jamie looking bemused at me. Perhaps I should not have come to church on this occasion. Jamie was not the only one to notice my somewhat distant behaviour as, when it was time to leave, the vicar asked if I was alright.

He had taken my hand in his and looked searchingly into my eyes. Being a man of the cloth, I wondered if he had powers to read my mind and I was not so sure he would like what I had been thinking.

"I'm fine, thank you," I had managed to reply without sounding rude. That evening, however, I had decided that the following morning I would telephone the vicar and ask to meet with him.

Just after nine a.m., the next day, the telephone had rung. To my amazement, it was the vicar. How could he possibly know that I was going to call him? Again, I wondered whether he was able to read the mind of his parishioners.

The Reverend Richard Denby had been vicar of the local parish for over twenty years succeeding our previous elderly vicar, and friend, Jonathan who had sadly passed away. It was difficult for Richard, following in Jonathan's footsteps.

His predecessor had been a popular and much-loved vicar for many years. He had married Jamie and I and had baptised both of our children.

I had taken pity on Richard when he first arrived in the village. Being new to a small village parish, where everyone knew everyone else, might have been a little awkward. Inviting him and his wife Jenny, over for the occasional meal, we had got to know him well. Over the table, I would gossip a little and divulge little idiosyncrasies, relating to some of his parishioners. This was done kindly and in such a way as to enable Richard to avoid putting his foot into anything that might cause an individual upset.

"Hello, Ann, I just wanted to check you were alright? You seemed to be out of sorts yesterday in church."

Good on Richard to notice that one of his flock was out of sorts.

"Not really, Richard. I was about to phone you actually. I need to talk to you, but not over the phone."

I knew I must have sounded a bit secretive to him.

"That's OK. Would you like me to come to you or would you like to come to the vicarage?"

"Can I come to you? I feel we may not be disturbed so easily."

He probably thought that this was a strange request as I had never needed to visit the vicarage before. Anything that I had needed of the vicar was dealt with in the parish office.

This was also where committee meetings were held except, of course when we met in the local pub.

The Fleece Inn was an old, sixteenth-century building that had small bar areas. The publican and his wife were both bell ringers in our church and they would gladly reserve one of the small rooms for any of the social meetings. It was usually the one with the inglenook fireplace. The heat from the log fire and the ambience of the place made it difficult to leave after a meeting. The landlord could guarantee that a few drinks would be bought afterwards.

"I'm free at three o'clock this afternoon if that suits you, Ann?"

"Thank you, Richard, that sounds fine to me."

The rest of that morning had been a muddled one. Every chore I did seemed to take me longer to do. My thoughts were in such disarray that I had been clumsy and had broken two pieces of my best china. Normally, I would have scolded myself, but on this occasion, I didn't care. Picking up the broken pieces, I had cut my finger and hadn't noticed it straight away. It was only when I had picked up the tea towel, to dry some dishes, that I saw spots of blood on the material. I fumbled around the kitchen cupboards looking for a plaster to dress the wound and dropped the first aid box onto the floor, spilling its contents and in doing so, I had broken a bottle of antiseptic solution, sending fragments of glass and patches of antiseptic over the kitchen floor.

"Bloody hell," I had sworn.

The aroma filled my nostrils and would later linger in the kitchen. I sat down on a chair and burst into floods of tears. Ignoring the telephone ringing, I folded my arms on the table and buried my head onto them and wailed pitifully; the sleeves of my sweater became wet from tears and mucous. Unable to locate anything to mop up my face, I sniffed into the air several times bringing my tears to their end. I remembered that the box of tissues was in the lounge and so went in search of them.

"Time for a walk in the garden," I said to myself.

Having taken a handful of tissues from the box, I went outside to take in some early spring air.

The garden, at this time of year, is full of mystery. There are swollen bulbs, ready to burst into blooms of colour; the early ones are already beginning to show. I stop to admire some of my favourite ones, like the clusters of pure white snowdrops and golden crocuses. The birds sing happily and some fly in from the hedgerows to feed from the table while others search for the raw materials for nest building. There is still a chill in the air and I have forgotten to put on a coat. Quickening my pace, I walk to the bottom of the garden and stop to look at the fruit trees. Their branches, covered in small buds, are also waiting for the warmth of spring to entice new growth and the promise of fruit. I know that everything in the garden is awakening to a new life and that I will see it for the very last time.

That afternoon, and feeling a little apprehensive, I set off to meet with the vicar.

It was a good walk into the village and I had always enjoyed it. I was unlikely to meet with anyone until I reached the village itself so had time to think about what I would say to Richard when I met him.

It's funny how I have always done this. If ever I was to meet someone new, I would think beforehand as to what I might say. More often than not it didn't really help because I would have forgotten my thoughts as soon as introductions had been made and pleasantries completed.

Richard had seen me approach from the window of his office. He had been sitting at his desk, which faced the window and overlooked his front garden. Anyone coming through the gate, to walk the short distance up the garden path, would be met at the door before they had time to ring the doorbell. It was his way of being friendly.

"Hello, Ann, come on in; what a lovely day it is; almost spring-like, don't you think?"

"Yes it is lovely, thank you."

He ushered me into his study and offered me a cushioned seat next to his own, but to the side of his desk. The sun was pouring in through the window and blinding me. Richard quickly pulled the blind to shut out part of the dazzling light. He turned his chair towards me, away from the desk, creating a less formal situation. Leaning forward and smiling, he was about to say something.

"Richard, I'm dying," I had blurted out, not giving him the chance to say anything, "the cancer has come back and cannot be cured."

His face was one of disbelief. It was obviously not what he had expected to hear me say.

"Ann, I am so sorry. I had no idea…"

How could he have had? I had only just found out myself. Now I find myself apologising to him.

"It's not your fault, but that's why I wanted to see you."

Richard leant over and took my cold hands in his. The warmth of his hands was comforting and I was happy for him to keep them there. I had never experienced Richard being so tactile. I had only ever shaken his hand briefly, coming out of the church after a service. He may have expected me to cry but I explained to him that I had cried all that morning.

"I feel so angry with everyone and everything," I went on, "I don't want to die. Why can't I live? Where is God now? Why can't he stop this?"

His eyes looked sad as he contemplated a response.

"I will not have all the answers for you, Ann, but I will try to help you make sense of some of your thoughts. It would be wrong for me to say that I understand when I do not, when I cannot. No one can truly understand your feelings unless they themselves experience what you are going through."

Richard paused and gently rubbed my cold hands. I had not noticed their blue tinge, let alone felt the cold. Looking into his eyes, I knew that he genuinely cared.

"Jesus, however, does know what you are going through as he himself experienced the same feelings, calling on God when he thought he had forsaken him in his hour of need."

I had momentarily forgotten about the crucifixion of Jesus. I didn't know how to respond and Richard seemed to understand this.

"Let's put God to one side for now and talk in confidence as friends, Ann. We have known each other for a long time; I will never forget how kind you were when my wife and I moved into this parish. I would like you to try and tell me what you are feeling."

It was a difficult process but, in the end, I managed to tell him of my anger towards my friend who had survived cancer. I told him of other cancer patients I had nursed, those who had responded to treatment and were now cured. Most important of all, I confessed of my doubt in the existence of God but in the same sentence was concerned that if he did exist, would my sins be forgiven and would I go to heaven? Having thought about my last sentence, I realised that it made no sense.

We smiled simultaneously as we realised the ridiculousness of what I had just confessed to him.

"Ann, I want you to put your trust in me. You already know that what we discuss will be between ourselves and I hasten to add, God. I will continue to pray for you and with you when you feel that you are ready. I will always be here for you when you want me. Try not to look too far ahead but take one day at a time. You have a good family and lots of friends that I know will want to help and support you. If you will let me, I would like to help you too both as your vicar, but more importantly, as your friend. Between us, I believe we can find some of the answers that you are looking for."

For the remainder of our meeting, we talked about cancer and I told him what the doctor had said. We discussed the family and he asked me how Jamie and the children had taken the news.

"With your permission, Ann, I would like to speak to Jamie. I want him to know that I am here for both him and the children as well."

I was glad that he had suggested this. It made me realise that I had been selfish as I had not given my family any thought on the matter.

On subsequent meetings with Richard, I had discussed openly about my fear of death. In the weeks that followed, I became less angry, becoming more focussed on the family and their needs, even talking about my own funeral arrangements. I did not want to leave this until it was too late. I had found comfort from my meetings with Richard.

Sometimes we would walk in the vicarage garden together, enjoying the spring sunshine, or stroll down into the village. On some occasions, we had sat quietly in church together. It would take several meetings with him before I was able to pray with meaning again and to eventually find some peace in my heart.

About a month to the date of my first meeting with Richard, it had been the anniversary of my mother's death. As was the usual custom, I gathered some late spring flowers from the garden and took a stroll to the cemetery at the rear of St Edmond's Church. Every year I had done this, except for when Jamie and I had been away from home either for work or on holiday. On these occasions, I would try and visit in the days preceding the anniversary, or on our return.

This particular morning, however, I had been in good spirits. The weather had been favourable, the sun was shining and there was warmth in the air.

I had met with Richard several times in the previous weeks and it had helped.

My annual visit, to lay flowers at the family grave, was something I now did on my own. Attitudes towards visiting the graves of dead people vary within families, as was the case in my own. Jamie, who shared similar beliefs to me, did not see the necessity to visit graves. Mathew was also of the same opinion. Lottie would occasionally accompany me but never expressed an opinion either way. This she stopped doing after her grandmother's death. Life circumstances had changed; both children were busy individuals and often away from home.

As I entered the churchyard, I looked around and became aware that, on this occasion, I would be alone. An elderly lady was just leaving through the back gate. I watched as she placed dead flowers in the compost bin, by the side of the gate, before leaving. Collecting water from the outside tap, in one of the rusty cans that were provided, I proceeded to the family plot.

Some of the graves were kept neat and tidy while others appeared to be neglected. This often made me feel sad. The family grave was neither of these. Sometimes the grass would look as if it needed some attention and the headstone, which was carved in the shape of a book, would benefit from a good scrubbing. At other times, when I had visited, I had removed dead flowers not knowing who had placed them there. I would only assume that my mother, or my brother, had friends that still visited here. There were times when I found that fresh flowers had been recently placed in one of the two glass vases that were half-buried in the ground.

On this particular morning's visit, I found fresh flowers in one of the two vases. A bunch of small, out-of-season, red roses. As was usually the case, there was no label to identify the person who had placed them there. I knelt down on a plastic bag that I always carried in my handbag. I noticed that the headstone in front of me had also been recently cleaned or certainly since my last visit, which had been just before Christmas. This was when I had laid the annual holly wreath. *Who,* I thought to myself, *would have done this kind thing?*

Looking around the cemetery, to make sure I was still alone, I began to speak softly.

"Hello, Mum," I said, "I do miss you and Dougie, of course. I miss you both too, Nannie and Granddad. I hope you are all happy together wherever you are."

The carved headstone bore the names of my grandparents on the first 'page' and on the second was my mother's name and with it, my brother Douglas' whose ashes had also been scattered over the grave. Both pages were inscribed with words of love and wisdom, as well as the dates each had departed from this world. Dutifully, I placed the spring flowers in the second vase and filled it with the water from the can. The can leaked and water dribbled out from the rusty holes. I scolded myself, as I had forgotten that I'd made a promise on my last visit to donate some new ones.

I wondered how long the flowers would last as the churchyard was often visited by deer from the woods behind the church. They feasted on the flowers and plants that were left on the graves of loved ones. Over the years, fences had been erected but this had not stopped the deer from getting in. Local residents, with the church committee, had given up on trying to keep them out. It was so peaceful; all was quiet, except for the sound of birds singing from the trees and I looked around me to make sure that I was still alone.

I wanted to tell my mother and grandparents that I was shortly to join them. I asked them to be there for me when the time came and I confessed, to them, that I felt frightened.

On my feet again, I collected the last remaining flowers and watering can and followed the stony path, around the corner, to where my aunt and uncle were laid to rest. This was one of those graves that had become a little overgrown and I often felt guilty for not spending time tidying it up as I had our own. If it hadn't been for the many part-time gardeners, employed by the church over the years, it would indeed have been a disgrace. A small vase in the ground was difficult to locate as it was filled with dead leaves. Taking it out, I rubbed the vase with my hand to take off the dry dirt. Filling it with water, I placed it back in position and put the remaining flowers into it. Under my breath, I apologised for not looking after the plot as I should have.

When I had finished, I stood up, perhaps a little too quickly as I immediately felt very dizzy and fell back onto my knees to stop myself from falling right over. A gentleman's voice spoke from behind me.

"Are you alright? Can I help you?"

I turned to see who it was that had spoken to me but the brilliant sun was shining directly into my eyes. Bringing my hand up to shield my dazzled eyes from the sun, I saw the figure of a tall gentleman. He seemed to be dressed in a long black coat and was wearing a large-brimmed black hat. I could not be sure but I thought he wore a white collar around his neck. The voice had surprised me as I thought I had been alone. Quickly, I established that he must be a visitor to the church.

"That's very kind, thank you, but I think I am fine now."

The man put out his hand to assist me to my feet. I was reluctant to take the hand of a stranger. Rather awkwardly, I managed to slowly stand up. I turned towards the stranger and was amazed that, as I did so, he had disappeared. I looked around the churchyard but did not see anyone else there. *How strange,* I thought to myself. My dizzy spell had now gone and I wanted to leave quickly and get home, in case it returned.

Replacing the watering can, I left through the gate by which I had entered. Walking home, I could not think of anything else but what I thought I had seen and heard. Could I have seen the ghost of the same man that I had seen before?

I decided that I would mention it to Richard when I next saw him. This was the last time I would be able to visit the churchyard.

As my cancer became progressively worse and I no longer had the strength to leave the house, Richard would continue to visit me in my home.

# Chapter 12

Coming back to the present, my thoughts turn to Lottie. If Lottie is pregnant, as I suspect she is, then she cannot be many weeks along and she is likely to be tired, both from working her shifts and looking after me. Men are less intuitive beings and Jamie was unlikely to notice the changes in her, as I had, so, for now, I will keep my intuitions to myself. Maybe she doesn't know herself yet or perhaps she is unsure whether to tell me or not. I muse over this to myself.

Jamie turns on to his other side and almost falls from the bed and this makes me giggle.

"I told you so," I jest.

Smiling, he gets up and stretches and this is instantly followed by a deep groan.

Taking in his semi nakedness, I admire his torso. His upper body is in good shape. Muscles are evident in both his arms and chest. He has always looked after himself. He's always been a competitive sportsperson, who, to this day, still enjoys a game of squash. In his youth, he has enjoyed playing the game of rugby; from school to university and then for our local team. Now he is just content to watch the game and support while others play.

Mathew had also enjoyed playing rugby and we had supported whichever team he had been playing for at that given time.

Bending down to retrieve his dressing-gown, which had fallen to the floor, instigated a second groaning sound. Standing upright again, I watched him as he rubbed the ache in his left side.

"Guess we're not as young as we use to be?" he remarked, "I remember the days when we had plenty of room in a single bed." He smiled and bent over a little more cautiously to kiss me. "How are you feeling this morning, my love?"

"Happy to see another day," I smiled.

"And the pain?"

I reassured him that I was OK and could manage a little longer before I would need my next dose of pain relief.

"Don't forget, your brother is coming today, but only if you are up to it?" He looks at me for a reaction.

"I am looking forward to seeing him again." Jamie knows my fondness for my brother.

"Perhaps it'd be better if he comes alone though, I think I will suggest it to him when he phones later."

"No, please don't, I'm looking forward to seeing Jean as well and catching up with news of the family, especially the twins. We women like to boast about our children and their attributes," I teasingly add.

"Alright, but only if you're sure." Smiling, he bends over and drops a kiss on to my forehead.

My only living brother, John, has lived in Australia for many years with his wife Jean and their two daughters, Ruth and Elizabeth. They had emigrated. It had not been a light decision but John had been finding it hard to further his career.

Job opportunities were forth-coming as soon as their decision had been made. Outwardly, we were delighted for them but I really did not want John to go. It had been a difficult and sad time for me, saying good-bye to my brother not knowing whether we would see each other again. However, this new adventure had seen John prosper and he made an exceptional living in finance. I had never really understood his job but knew it had involved travelling the globe.

Five years ago, we had visited them for an extended holiday in sunny Oz and their hospitality had been generous. Observing their new way of life, it was easy to see that they had made the right choice. It was always lovely to catch up with the family.

Prior to this, we had only met on two other occasions and these were the funerals of our mother and then our brother Douglas.

Mum had died following a heart attack. It had been sudden and totally unexpected. At the time, her general health had seemed good. She never complained of anything. In fact, I often remarked that she was perfect and much too good for this world. I know it had been a strange thing to say but her goodness seemed to be appreciated and acknowledged by all who knew her. In the last few years, she had spent a lot of time helping the nuns in the priory. She took on sewing repairs and helped in the vegetable gardens. Mum could turn her hand to anything domestic. She was particularly fond of jam making. The priory gardens yielded an abundance of fruit that she would help to pick for her jam-making sessions. The final products would be sold in one of the local shops. I often wondered whether she ever considered joining the order of nuns at the priory. She had gentlemen callers who she would go out with but only as friends who shared similar interests with her. She never remarried after the death of my father.

"There would never be anyone that could take his place," she had once told me when I had asked her about a particular man friend. I wanted her to know that if she ever chose to marry again, it would always be with my blessing.

Her later life, however, would continue to be one of dedication to her work in the priory. Motherhood and grand-parenting were always at the top of her priorities. She doted on the grandchildren and was sorely missed by Mathew and Lottie.

Doug's racing car accident took place just one year after our mother's death. That same night, as I lay awake in my bed crying quietly, with Jamie asleep beside me, I saw again the ghost of the tall man. He was standing still at the bottom of the bed. His head was bowed. I had felt very frightened. My heart was thumping as if it could burst from my chest at any minute. I tried to call out to Jamie but my voice failed me. With my arms under the duvet, I tried to nudge Jamie awake. Deep in his sleep, there was no response. The apparition of the man stood for several seconds before turning to his right. Slowly, he walked towards the wall and disappeared. Flaying my arms and screaming out, eventually woke Jamie. He was startled. His response was to grab at my arms and shout at me.

"Calm down. What the hell has happened?"

"He was here again. The tall man. I tried to wake you. I was so scared."

"It's OK, it's just a dream."

"It was not a dream," I defended myself, angry at him because he never believed me.

Jamie did get up on this occasion and turned on the light. Naturally, there was nothing to see.

"Why does this keep happening to me? What can it mean?"

More gently now, Jamie tried to make sense of something he doesn't really believe in.

"I don't know why, but you have just lost your brother and it was only a year ago when Mum died. Your mind is probably playing tricks on you. Do you want to change sides of the bed?"

Adamant I was not having a dream, my response was frosty.

"No, it's OK, he never came as close to me as he sometimes does."

Sleep came just as the sun was rising and I knew we would both be tired the following day.

I had followed Doug's career with pride but could never watch him race live. Jamie took our children to support him and they always enjoyed their visits to the racing venues with their colourful atmospheres. Returning home, I would gladly listen to their accounts of the race and their imaginative descriptions of an exciting race day; the smoke and smell of motor oil, the engine revs of the cars screeching around the track. It all sounded very exciting and I was glad that they had enjoyed the experience.

Both of our children were very fond of their uncle. He would spoil them with expensive gifts from his travels. They would boast to their friends of his successes. It was fortunate that the children had never been invited to attend any qualifying races as Doug needed to concentrate and preferred to be alone.

It was on one of these occasions when the accident had happened and he had lost his life.

Doug had never married but did however have many lady friends. He enjoyed the bachelor life. Travelling around the world and living out of a suitcase. He seldom needed to book hotels as his many friends would insist that he accept their hospitality and accommodation. He was a charming and popular man, not unlike our father, and had enjoyed the company of many a famous person. When we were with him, he would take great pleasure in introducing us to someone famous.

The accident had happened on the final lap of a qualifying race. The inquest that followed had ruled it to be an accidental death due to an unfortunate set of circumstances when he had miss-judged his speed on the final bend of a very wet track. The crash site was a mess and we were told that his injuries were most severe and that he had died instantly. Fortunately, no one else had been injured.

John had flown across for the funeral, but could not stay for any length of time due to his work commitments at that time.

With Christmas nearly here, my brother John with his wife Jean had decided to return to England and spend the holidays with their daughter Ruth and son-in-law Ian, who lived in Devon.

Ruth had met Ian when he was holidaying in Australia. They fell head over heels in love and Ruth decided to return to England to be with Ian. One year later, they were married.

The twins were born two years later. The little girls had been born prematurely and had spent their first five weeks in a neonatal unit. Ruby needed ventilation support for several days. Her sister Sara was the stronger of the two. Both were fed through nasal tubes until they were able to suckle.

With her parents in Australia, Jamie and I became surrogate parents to Ruth and gave her as much support as we could. John or Jean would phone regularly for news until both babies were stable. The day they came home, Lottie and I decorated their house with pink ribbons and balloons.

John and Jean have managed two visits so far and this would be their third. Although I am reasonably sure their visit, at this time, was legitimate (even though they had visited back in the Spring), I couldn't help having a suspicious feeling that they wanted to see me one last time too and I loved them for it.

"Guess we had better get a move on," Jamie assisted me to the bathroom and guided me onto the toilet seat. My weak emaciated frame could not hold me on my feet for any length of time. Since my condition had deteriorated, I was in need of more help with personal and intimate care. At first, I felt a little embarrassed but as I became weaker, I no longer had the energy or will to care. Was I being selfish to expect someone so close to help with such personal activities of daily living? Had I given enough thought to Jamie's feelings and those of my children and my best friend Jill? I continually ask myself these questions.

"This is a bit humiliating," I had remarked on one occasion.

"Why do you say that? I think after all these years together I have seen everything there is to see." I knew Jamie was trying to make light of it all, and in a way, it was reassuring.

Back in my bed, he helped me to undress and tenderly proceeded to wash me. The warm, rose-scented water was refreshing. There was still a little embarrassment on my part because of my breast disfigurement. Jamie had never shied away, he was always tender and loving towards me. He praised the surgeon on more than one occasion, believing that he had done a great job.

The scaring was thick and the overall appearance to me was ugly.

"You must give it time to heal properly."

His words had been full of encouragement.

"I still love you, you know. Nothing will ever change that!"

Could anyone be as lucky as I was, faced with such a hideous body, to have someone like Jamie to love me, to shower me with comforting words of support? Without him, I don't think I would have got through those difficult dark days or indeed, the darker ones I now endure…

Dried and dressed casually, in a pale blue floral cotton shirt, I rested back on the freshly plumped up pillows. Gently, Jamie combed my hair. The soft, baby-like hair was now very thin on my scalp. He would never let me see the hairbrush, which I knew would hold the remnants of hair from even the gentlest of brushing. Carefully, he added a floral broad band of material, which was gently elasticated. It fitted well around my head, covered much of my hair and was, thankfully, easy to put on.

"Not a pretty sight, am I?" I say with a smile.

"Don't run yourself down, my Ann, you're far prettier than you think," Jamie replies, and he kisses me on my head, "I love you lots."

"Seriously though, you must say if it gets too much for you, I will go into St. Luke's if you want me to." The hospice had told me that I could go in, at any time, if ever I changed my mind.

Jamie knows my feelings on this subject. I sometimes believe that he can read my mind.

"This is what we both want, so no more talk about it," I am sweetly reprimanded, "I had better get to the bathroom before the others wake up and the queue starts!"

After breakfast, everyone went about their own business. Jamie went to his study to catch up with some work. Lottie went home to see Pete, with a promise to return for Uncle John's visit later that afternoon when we knew of the forthcoming visit, Pete had insisted that he would organise the meal for the evening.

"Only if we can pay you the going rate," Jamie had insisted.

"You know that's not necessary, I am family, you know." We would always be grateful for Pete's culinary contributions.

Mathew was the last to get up and make his appearance. He ate his breakfast from a tray, sitting by my side. In between mouthfuls, munching on a substantial bowl of cereal, he told me of his plans to meet Abbie at the station that evening. She had some holiday due and because of Mathew's leave, would spend Christmas here in Sussex.

Abbie's parents lived a few miles over the border, in Surrey, and she would spend the nights with them and the days with Mathew. I wondered if Abbie's parents were waiting, like us, to hear the sound of wedding bells. After all, Mathew and Abbie had been friends since university and now they lived together.

"None of my business," I reprimand myself.

There was a knock at the door and Mathew got to his feet to answer it. Jill was her usual cheerful self this morning, and even more excited on seeing Mathew answer the door. From the noise they were making, I could visualise Mathew lifting Jill off her feet with a generous hug, such are the close relationships we all enjoy.

Voices that were loud and cheerful, now went noticeably quieter as Jamie joined them in the hallway. I knew that they were most probably talking about me. With little strength available, to fight any anger I was feeling, I managed to ignore them.

"Morning, Ann and how are you today? Jamie say's you had a good night."

If Jamie said that I did, then I guess I must have, but my reply will be one of civility.

"Yes I did, thank you. I am still having disturbing and confusing dreams though."

"I increased your morphine last night so it was probably due to that."

She didn't need to elaborate on her comments. She respected my medical knowledge and knew I would understand the possible side effects from the increased amount of morphine I had been given.

"Can I go back to the smaller dose this morning? The pain is not so great and I want to be awake for John when he arrives later this afternoon."

"Yes, of course, you can," she added, "if you need me to come back earlier than usual, this evening, for the night dose then I can, as long as you're sure you can cope today?"

"Thanks, Jill."

Assessment and pleasantries completed, she left. I was in no doubt that she had a busy day ahead of her. After all, I was not her only patient.

Respecting my privacy, Mathew had left the room for the consultation with my nurse. Having carried his tray to the kitchen, and consultation having finished, he promptly returned and sat in the chair by my side again.

"Mum," he says, "can I ask you something?"

"What is it, love?" I can see he is deliberating as to whether to ask his question or not.

"How do you feel about Christmas this year? Shall we ignore it?"

"Certainly not," I quickly add, "I just haven't given it much thought," a lie. "Why don't you bring down the decorations from the attic and decorate the tree before Uncle John arrives this afternoon?"

"Is that what you want, Mum?"

"Yes, I do. We must make some arrangements for gifts too. You do the decorating while I have a rest, and then we can talk some more."

"Birthday gifts first," he says cheekily, tapping the side of his nose.

A quick kiss on my cheek and with a bounce in his step, like a child, he almost ran up the stairs.

Who am I to deny the biggest celebration of the year to my family? After all, was it not one of my favourite times of the year? I only pray that I will live to see one last Christmas.

Sleep came easily, and in my dreams, I saw a Christmas from the past.

It is Christmas day in my grandparents' house. The sitting room is decorated with lengths of coloured, twisted, streamers. Attached at each corner of the room, they meet in the centre, where they are secured together, leaving short lengths to dance in the drafts of the old cottage. A Christmas tree with lights of bright bold colours sits on a table under the window. How I had loved this room, probably because we were only allowed in it on special occasions, Christmas being one of them.

Everyone is there. Nannie and Aunty Dotty are sitting together on the couch, deep in conversation. Mum is busy laying the table and using Nannie's best china, taken carefully from the sideboard. Granddad and Uncle Harry are standing by the lit fire. In their hands, they each hold a large glass of cider. On the floor, my brothers and I are playing with our new toys.

That year I had received a new doll. It was dressed in pretty pale pink clothes with a coat and hat and booties to match, and I remembered I had seen my mum knitting these very things, in the days leading up to Christmas.

Everyone is smiling and yet the atmosphere is subdued.

My eyes search for the missing person, who I cannot see, and I am suddenly full of sadness. My father is not there because he is overseas. Korea was now at war.

My memories of my father are few. I knew he had been a soldier and had fought bravely in the Second World War. I could remember being carried on his shoulders, and I always thought of him as a very strong man.

One harvest, I had helped to pick the apples, in the orchard, for cider making. I would boast to my brothers that I could reach the best apples from the top of the tree. Cider making was a tradition in our family. After gathering the apples, I would watch as the process of preparing the apples, by grinding them before the pressing, began. The smell of apple juice being squeezed through the press, and hessian cloth has always stayed with me. The locals used to say that my grandfather and Uncle Harry had made the best cider in the village.

One of my clearest memories of my father was his singing voice. It was beautiful. He had often been cajoled into singing, by family and friends at parties and events. Everyone would join in and I would pretend to know the lyrics and attempt to sing along with them.

Another one of my delights was to persuade my father, and the menfolk to blow out their cigarette smoke and turn it into rings in the air, and with my brothers, we'd try to put a finger through the ring before it disappeared.

Memories of the day that he died are very vague, almost non-existent. I knew something was wrong, but being so young I did not understand, and I had probably been shielded by the adults. It was some years later that I would come to understand that he never returned from his second deployment to Korea, that he had been killed in action.

How proud he would have been to have known Mathew, to have seen him following in his footsteps.

The sound of something smashing on the floor woke me abruptly from my sleep and dreams.

"Sorry, Mum, I thought I was being quiet. Until I dropped a bauble. I think it's one of your favourite ones too, sorry."

How silly to have 'favourite' insignificant things. Material things are of no importance now and perhaps they never should have been.

"Don't worry, Mathew, it really doesn't matter."

"You were smiling in your sleep," he teases, "Was it a good dream?"

"I was dreaming of a Christmas, long ago, when I was a small child."

Mathew hurries to my side as I try to lift my head from the pillow. Supporting my shoulders, he places another pillow behind my head and I wince in pain.

"Sorry, Mum, did I hurt you?"

"It's OK, just a little stiff from being in one position."

"Were all your Christmases happy ones, Mum?"

"The ones that I can remember were."

Looking across the room, I can see the tree already decorated and it looks beautiful.

"You're just in time for the big switch-on," Mathew states excitedly.

"Oh no, let's save that for later, when everyone's here."

"You missed lunch, Mum. Can I get you something?"

I shake my head in refusal, but it's no use; Jamie has entered the room and I know that I will have to persevere to try to eat something now.

The Christmas tree is beautifully decorated in red and gold. Expensive, fragile, baubles hang with the old family favourites, including those made at school, by both Mathew and Lottie. Some are looking tired, but all are much too precious to throw away. At the top of the tree is the angel. My guardian angel, as I used to call it.

My father had bought the angel for my mother, to celebrate their first Christmas in their own home. Mum had used it every year until Mathew was born, and then it was passed down to me. Looking at it now, I wonder whether I will be able to pass it on to Lottie soon?

Lottie and Pete arrive, just as the clock chimes for four o'clock, laden down with plastic boxes of food, from Pete's restaurant kitchen.

"Hi, Mum, how are you feeling?" Lottie greets me with a kiss.

"All good, thanks. What do you think of the tree?" I turn her attention away from me. "Don't you think Mathew's done a good job?"

"It's beautiful, Matt. The angel is a bit wonky though," Lottie jests.

Climbing on a chair, Mathew attempts to make the angel look a little less drunk!

"That's better, Matt," she reassures him with a kiss on his cheek. "Can you give Pete a hand to bring in more food from the car? I think he's planning to feed the five thousand!"

More boxes and packages of food are carried through to the kitchen.

"Thank you, Pete, for doing all the cooking. I don't know how we would have managed."

A jesting voice rings out from the kitchen as Mathew informs everyone that he could have opened a few tins of something.

Pete gives me his usual hug and a kiss.

"It's my way of helping out and don't forget how much I enjoy the cooking."

The young adults have always got on well together. I look forward to seeing Abbie this evening, and then my family will be complete.

Shortly after six o'clock, John and Jean arrive. Emotions of excitement mingle with relief that he is here and I start to cry. John and I hold each other and I do not want to let him go.

"Come on, Ann, let us all have a look in," Jamie shakes John by the hand but then pulls John towards him and they also hug. Kisses and hugs are the order of the day. There's not a dry eye in the room.

Reaching out, I touch John's hand and dutifully he moves a chair closer to me.

"Oh, John, it's so lovely to see you and looking so well. It must be the grandchildren that keep you both looking so young. Tell us the news of everyone?"

Typically, being a proud grandfather, he starts by telling us how wonderful the little ones are. Reaching into his pocket, he pulls out a paper wallet containing photographs and distributes them around the room.

"Such beautiful little girls," I comment. The photograph shows them wearing identical outfits.

"Bit of a handful at times but great fun," he replies, "Ruth and Ian are both well and of course send you their love. They thought it best not to bring the children out so late. Young parents these days have something called a routine," he chuckles, "not like that in our days, was it, sis?"

A delightful hour was spent exchanging news. Lizzie, their second daughter, had remained in Australia to share Christmas with her new boyfriend.

"We really wanted Lizzie to come with us but this new boyfriend of hers wanted her to spend time with his family. We won't be surprised if there is another wedding soon."

By now, I was beginning to feel very tired and uncomfortable. Pete called from the dining room to say that supper was ready, I insisted they all went in, and that I was quite happy to be left alone. Jamie brought me a tray with some soup and fruit jelly. Everyone tried so hard to tempt me with small morsels of food.

"Try and eat a little, love, got to keep your strength up, especially now that John is here."

Jamie left me with the food. My sense of smell and taste had almost diminished. Scooping a little soup on to the spoon was difficult enough, let alone bringing the food to my mouth. More food ended up in the napkin than in my mouth. Retching as the warm liquid entered my mouth, I quickly gave up. I tried a little jelly, but that too just made me feel sick. Using a straw, I attempted a few mouthfuls of Complan and decided that that was enough for now. So far, I had managed to feed myself and could not bear the thought of someone else feeding me.

Jill had made it quite clear that if I became dehydrated, I would have to have an intravenous infusion, and that would mean being admitted to the hospital.

Exhausted, I lay back slowly onto the pillow. The pain is becoming more severe and I know I will soon be ready for some more morphine. Jill would be here at her usual time of nine o'clock, so I would not have to wait much longer.

Sounds of laughter, coming from the dining room, reminded me of family gatherings we had enjoyed over the years. Such happy memories I have. I could almost hear my grandmother's voice.

"Remember, Ann, God gave us memories that we might have roses in December."

"Thank you, Nannie, where ever you are."

Supper was finished and Jean helped Lottie to clear the table.

"Compliments to the chef," John was rubbing his stomach in appreciation.

Everyone seated themselves back in the lounge and coffee was served by Lottie, with the help of Jean. Jamie, the perfect host, then offered brandy to those that wanted.

"OK, let's turn on the tree lights," an excited Mathew exclaimed, as he made his way to the switch. "Ready, Mum?" he asked and proceeded to count backwards from ten.

Lights on and the room appeared magical. Not only were there tree lights but Mathew had put more lights around the fireplace and the window. I hadn't noticed him hanging these this morning.

"Mathew, it's lovely," I beamed. Looking around the room at everyone's face, I could see they were relieved at my reaction. "Happy Christmas, everyone, I know there is another week to go but it's been so lovely having everyone here tonight."

Jean came and sat with me. In her hand, she held a parcel.

"Tomorrow is your birthday, but I can't wait till then. John and I have put this together for you. I hope you will like it."

Fumbling with the bright red wrapping paper, Lottie came to my assistance. Under the paper was a second layer. This time, some green tissue paper.

"Jean loves wrapping presents, it looks a bit like pass the parcel," John remarked teasingly.

Removing the second layer of tissue paper, a small album was revealed. My fingers worked to open the first page and I was overwhelmed by the contents. Each page was filled with old black and white photographs of my family, some with tattered edges and others with stains. Through watery eyes, I could see distorted pictures of people I once knew. Lottie took a handful of tissues from the box and handed them to me. Wiping away the tears, I could clearly see each character, my grandparents, Auntie Dotty and Uncle Harry, the cottages as they use to be, pictures taken in the garden and pictures taken in the orchard. There was even one of the old cider press, that was kept in the shed at the bottom of the garden. Some of the pictures were of village scenes, including those of the church and the priory. There was a picture, taken inside the village hall, where a party for children was taking place. There were two photos of Mum and Dad, and another depicting Dad wearing his army uniform. There were also three photos of John, Doug and myself as young children.

"Why had I not seen these before?" I ask myself.

"Mum gave some to me when we emigrated," John was reading my mind. "Some were in an old shoebox that I took from Mum's house after she died. I didn't really take any notice of the contents until we got home," he continued.

This was a real boost to me. From somewhere inside, I found a hidden strength. I did not want to put the album down, turning page after page and then going back to start again, such was my fascination and enjoyment of the album. John helped me to identify those individuals and occasions that I did not recognise. There were photographs of local people from the village and workers from the estate. He also had a better memory than me when it came to dating some of the photographs. This was probably because he had been older than I. There was one photograph taken at Christmas time, easily identifiable with the trimmings and decorated tree.

On closer inspection, I experienced a déjà vu. The photograph showed the same Christmas that I had dreamt about just that afternoon. Everyone was there, that I had seen in my dream, and wearing the same clothes.

"Look, Ann, do you remember that Christmas. There you are in the front of the picture standing next to Nan. You're holding your doll. That's me and Doug," John pointed to the individuals.

"I don't really remember it," I confessed, not wanting to share my strange dream of earlier.

"It was the first Christmas without our dad," he continued. "I remember Mum trying to make it a happy day for us, but I did see her crying later that day."

"John," I ask, a little confused, "if we are all in the picture, then who took the photograph?"

"That would be Nan's friend, Sister Mary. I don't think she had any family of her own. Being of similar age to our mum, I think Nan looked to her as one of the family."

"I don't remember her at all," I quickly add, "is there a photograph of her?"

"Let me see," John moved closer to my side and began scrutinising the pictures. "Yes, look, there she is," he exclaimed, pointing to a picture that had been taken outside the village hall. "She is standing there, next to our mum. I can't tell you what the occasion was though."

I studied the faded picture closely. There were a small group of young ladies. Each held a baby of various sizes. The lady standing next to our mum was indeed wearing a nurse's uniform. In her arm, she held a large bouquet of flowers.

I had no intention of telling anyone that I had seen this woman in a dream; they are bound to say that somewhere in the back of my mind I must have remembered her.

Casually, I enquired as to what had become of her.

111

"Not absolutely sure, Ann. I don't remember seeing much of her when we moved to our new house. When Doug fell out of the tree and had a deep cut to his knee, he was seen by a different nurse. That must have been a couple of years after that photo was taken because I think Doug may have been a couple of years older than that."

John went quiet. I thought he was doing some mathematical calculations in his head.

"All so long ago," he concluded.

All of this excitement had taken its toll on me and I was becoming weary again and struggled to stop myself from yawning. It was Jamie that called the evening to a halt.

"I think we have all had enough excitement for one day."

I know he is referring this remark particularly to me. John and Jean say their goodbyes to everyone. More hugs and kisses, delaying the proceedings.

"We will see you tomorrow, Ann, on your birthday, but will only stay for a short time. We plan to travel to Devon after lunch. Ruth and Ian are expecting us for supper and we don't know what the traffic situation will be like."

Wrapping my arms around his neck, I do not want to let him go.

"Thank you both for coming today. I know you must be anxious to see your family again, as I am sure they are to see you. I love you both and will look forward to seeing you tomorrow before you go, even if it's only for a little while."

Everyone moves towards the front door. There are further lingering hugs in the hallway and then they are gone. Next, there are goodnight hugs from Lottie and Pete before they too take their leave for their own home.

Mathew excuses himself and leaves to meet Abbie from the train.

The house is suddenly very quiet. Jamie pours himself another brandy and comes to sit with me.

"You must be exhausted, my love, and don't try to pretend you're not. I know the pain is also getting bad because I can see it in your face," Jamie is always observant when it comes to me.

"It has been such a lovely day. I have enjoyed having everyone here. I hope I can manage tomorrow as well."

Jamie leans over to kiss me.

"A good night's sleep is what you need. One without those silly dreams you keep having," I know he is mocking me.

"Believe me, I don't want to have any more strange dreams, especially about the past," I deliberately mislead him. The truth is, I have a strong desire to revisit the past. There are too many unanswered questions. They must be important enough to merit my attention and I want to understand why.

Picking up the photo album, Jamie studies some of its contents.

"It was good of John to put together these old photos for you. You were a pretty little thing when you were little," he smiles at me, "I think you take after your grandmother, but I can also see your mum in you too. She was a good looking woman as well."

There's a knock at the door and Jamie leaves to answer it. The familiar voice of Jill, enquiring after her patient, can be heard.

"She's had a busy day, Jill," Jamie's voice is a bit loud. I know he wants to make sure I can hear what is said but I also think he might have had one brandy too many!

Jill's arrival was a little earlier than expected and I was glad. With everyone gone, I realised the pain was getting quite severe. I noticed she was looking very tired, and I hoped that I was her last patient of the day. Determined not to take up too much of her time, I suggested a quick injection and that we leave everything else until tomorrow.

"Slow down, Ann. Do you want me to lose my job or something? Anyway, I was hoping to have a little quality time with my friend. First things first."

She undoes her bag and takes out the instruments for my examination. I know that these things must be done, but I am getting quite desperate now, for my morphine, and it is becoming difficult to be civil. Jill appears to be taking her time and lacks concentration.

"Are you OK, Jill?" I feel obliged to enquire.

"That's my line," she replied jokingly. "I'm fine. Just had a bit of a strange sort of day," she added.

"Anything you can tell me about, or is it all confidential?" I enquire.

"Not really confidential, if I don't mention certain details. I would like to share something with you though but first, I must care for my favourite patient here."

Examination completed thoroughly, I observed my nurse draw up the ampoule of morphine. Methodically expelling the air from the syringe and checking the prescription again for accuracy, before injecting it into my vein. Like a child waits for sweeties, so I waited eagerly for my injection of morphine. With her back to me, I watch as she packs her things tidily away in her bag. Picking up my soft baby hairbrush, she returns and sits by my side. Removing my headband, she gently begins to brush my hair. The morphine begins to take effect and the pain diminishes. My body relaxes. Jill gently lifts my head and shoulders. Supporting my upper body, she continues brushing the back of my hair. When she has finished, she turns and plumps the pillows before gently releasing me from her support. Next, she moves to the bottom of my bed and loosens the blankets to expose my feet. Moving to the small table at the head of the bed, which contains an assortment of pills and creams, she selects a bottle of pink moisturising lotion. Pouring a generous amount of rose perfumed liquid on to her hands, she kneels down and gently begins to massage my feet.

"Oh, Jill, you really don't have to do this," I am not in the least bit embarrassed as it feels so good.

"Shh! Just close your eyes and relax."

With the pain almost completely gone, I can easily relax.

My eyes remain closed as the massage comes to the end. Jill leaves me briefly, making her way to the kitchen to wash her hands. Returning swiftly, she once again sits down on the chair placed at my side.

"Thank you, Jill. I don't believe that treatment is part of your nursing duties. I don't think the NHS could afford it."

"I told you before, Ann, you are not just my patient and if circumstances were different, I know you would do the same for me."

We know each other very well.

"You must get off home, Jill. It's getting late and you look so tired."

With a broad grin, she suddenly perks up.

"I have a day off tomorrow, and anyway, David is out late this evening so there's no point rushing home."

She momentarily goes quiet and appears to be deep in thought.

"Come on then, Jill, tell me what's on your mind?"

"I shouldn't really talk about it, because it relates to a patient, however, I know I can trust you, Ann."

It was all sounding a little mysterious and I implored her to continue.

"I was wondering if you knew an elderly lady called Rosemary Thorne? She is in her late nineties and has been living in the Priory for many years."

The name did not ring any bells.

"I was asked to visit her," she continued. "She has terminal cancer and doesn't want to leave the Priory. The Sisters are happy to care for her but she needed to be assessed for pain control. Once the doctor had finished his examination and decided on a plan of care, he left. As I usually do, I stayed behind to get to know my patient a little better. She is a lovely lady. Sadly, though, she has some degree of dementia."

I am beginning to wonder why Jill feels the need to tell me about her patient. I continue to listen without interruption.

"Anyway, while I was talking to her she started to cry and she kept asking for forgiveness. She kept calling out for someone named Megan. I wouldn't have thought any more of it, but she mentioned someone else who she called Ruby."

My eyes were now open wide and Jill had got my full attention.

Jill continued, "I remembered your mother was called Ruby, and I also thought you had mentioned your

116

grandmother was called Megan. I'm sure it is all coincidental, but I thought I would just ask you anyway."

"Yes, Megan was my grandmother's name."

Jill had always been an inquisitive person and I didn't want to disappoint her.

"Mum worked in the priory before she died. I wonder if she would have known this Rosemary Thorne?" If she had, she never mentioned her to me. "I will ask John tomorrow if he knows anyone of that name. Do you know anything about her life?" I had thought that if I had more facts to offer John, that he may remember someone of that name.

"Sister Margaret told me that Rosemary was a spinster. She also said that for many years she had practised as a nurse. She was born here, in Sussex, and moved to London after the war. Apparently, she became a nurse tutor in one of the London hospitals. It was in her senior years that she came to live and work in the Priory."

My brain digests this new information and my heart begins to beat faster. I recall the strange dream that I had had. Could this be the same nurse that I had seen? Could she have been Nannie's friend? The same one that appears in the photograph.

Jamie knocks at the door before entering.

Apologising to me for taking so much of my time, and then to Jamie for keeping me up late, Jill gathers her things together and heads for the door.

"Don't forget, Ann, I have my day off tomorrow. I'm not sure who will be in to see you, but whoever it is, they know our plan of care. We have a new sabbatical community nurse. She's only been here for one week but has settled in quickly. I think she will be an asset to our team. Our workload has increased and there never seems enough time to spend with our patients, so I'm glad we have been allocated an extra pair of hands. I just wish it was a more permanent position. Anyway, I will still pop in for a piece of that birthday cake if that's all right?"

A quick but gentle hug and she is gone.

# Chapter 13

Jamie saw Jill to the door. They chatted for what seemed longer than the customary few minutes that it usually took to say goodbye. Their voices were low and I strained my ears to hear what they were talking about. Stupid me, I knew perfectly well that their conversation would be about my illness. I made the decision to question Jamie later as to what they had been talking about. Once again, I thought to myself, I had been denied the openness that I had insisted on from the very moment when I had first been told about my condition.

"Why did it take you so long to say goodbye to, Jill?"

From the way he looked at me, I could see that Jamie was angry. How many times have I opened my mouth without engaging my brain? Of course, he had every right to be angry, because, once again, I had doubted his loyalty.

"Ann, I promise you, we were not talking about your illness, other than Jill telling me that she had given you the larger dose of morphine this evening and to remind me to keep a closer eye on you. We discussed the side effects you were having and I needed to know if they might get worse."

I knew my reactions were totally unjustified. My suspicious thoughts, I knew were probably a result of the increased dose of morphine I had just been given. I felt so angry with myself. Why could I not control these feelings of insecurity?

"I'm so sorry, Jamie. I had no right to question you."

His facial expression began to relax again.

"Jill also wanted to be sure that you were up to her visiting you tomorrow, on your birthday. She was concerned it would be too much for you with the rest of the family here."

I was feeling slightly embarrassed now.

"Of course she must come, I hope you told her that. I would be so upset if she didn't. I am such a fool sometimes, I'm so sorry."

Jamie was smiling as he came closer to me. He bent over and kissed me.

"There is no need for any more apologies, we have passed all that. I promised you that we would not talk about your condition without you being present. We all have respect and admiration for the way you are coping."

Feeling quite sleepy now, and very relaxed, I reached out with what little strength I could muster to kiss him back, "I love you so much."

"And I love you too. It's time for you to get some sleep now. Is there anything I can get you?"

Jamie, as always, dutifully checked that I had everything to hand, including the small handbell.

"Promise me you won't try and get up by yourself. If you need anything at all, you must ring that bell."

From the emphasis on the word 'must' and the way he was looking at me, I knew that he was unsure whether I could be trusted.

"My life won't be worth living if Jill finds out that you insist on being on your own. I dread to think what she would say if you took a tumble."

"I promise to ring if I need anything," I knew it was highly unlikely that I would be able to get off the bed unaided, even if I tried.

"Will you stay with me until I fall asleep?" I asked.

"I would stay with you all night if you would let me."

"No, not tonight, my love. We both need to get a good night's sleep. It's going to be a busy day tomorrow!" I was concerned that Jamie was looking tired and I wondered again whether it was getting too much for him, taking care of me in our home.

The morphine was doing its job. The pain was more tolerable but it never seemed to go away completely. The feeling of drowsiness, and an improved sense of wellbeing, made it easier to cope with the pain. Death crept closer on a daily basis and I knew my time was running out. Some nights I was more eager for the end to come, but not tonight, for tomorrow I will see my beloved brother John. I knew that his visit will be the last opportunity I shall have to see him.

Jamie lay down next to me and gently manoeuvred himself so as not to cause me anymore discomfort. He positioned one arm so that I could nestle my head comfortably into his embrace. I found solace in the way that he held me so gently, like something very fragile that might easily break. With his free hand, he removed my scarf and then started to brush his fingers through my hair. My withered body began to relax, a combination of morphine, the closeness of Jamie and the subtle ticking of the clock enabled me to fall asleep easily. At some point, I could feel Jamie moving away from me. I could feel his warm lips upon my forehead and heard his whispered words.

"God bless you. I love you, my darling, with all my heart."

And then there was nothing.

How happy I suddenly felt.

With my eyes closed, I could visualise varying shapes, of beautiful mixtures of pastel colours, gently dancing in front of me. They move forward and surround me. Then the colours begin mixing together. The dance gathers momentum and new, more vibrant, bolder colours are made. The dancing colours start to change shape. They become more oblique and give the appearance of small rainbows. Looking down at myself, I seem to be dressed in a white, almost transparent, material. My body feels weightless and any movement I try to make using my arms and legs is slow. I cannot feel any pain at all. The colours that surround me begin to sparkle and my aura feels wonderful. This must be heaven, I decide.

Suddenly I am disturbed.

Somewhere in the distance, I can hear soft voices interspersed with the sound of laughter. I begin to feel annoyance towards the culprits. How dare they interrupt this pleasurable experience! The colours begin to fade and I do not want these feelings to go away. Whoever they are, they seem to have forgotten that I am unwell and need to sleep. Unable to arouse myself sufficiently to reprimand the individuals, that are acting thoughtlessly, I try to ignore them. The sounds come and go, and I am confused. I must act now before it gets out of hand.

"Please keep the noise down. I am trying to sleep."

Something suggests to me that it might be the children, who have come home late. It must be Saturday night because they seldom stay out on a weeknight. Perhaps they have brought their friends back home for coffee? The sound of muffled voices and laughter gets louder. It is coming from the kitchen and I can distinguish that someone is running water and the sound of crockery clanking together as if it is being washed in a sink.

Can't they see that I am sleeping? Why isn't their father here? He would surely tell them to keep the noise down.

The mantle clock chimes twice, it is trying to confuse me again but I know it is only one o'clock. I guess I shall have to be the unpopular parent tonight and tell them to keep the noise down. Jamie was the one who was always more lenient than I when it came to telling the children off.

"Have you forgotten what we were like when we were teenagers?" He would say to me. "They are only young once. No need to spoil their fun and anyway, it's not that late."

For Jamie to say this, when habitually he has to be in bed by eleven-thirty at the latest, it would amuse me.

However, the occasions when I had insisted he did get up to ask them to keep the noise down, he would end up joining in with their conversations and drinking coffee. This just encouraged them to stay up even later. Sometimes I would get very angry with all of them.

The room is in total darkness now, except for the dim light shining through the kitchen door, where it remains slightly ajar. As I get out of my bed, there is a sudden chill in the air and I shiver. Stepping carefully across the carpeted floor, so as not to bump into any furniture, the temperature continues to drop and it feels positively icy.

"It's going to be a frosty one tonight," I say to myself.

As I approach the kitchen door, it appears to open on its own accord. My senses become muddled. Looking into the room, I can see that it is not my kitchen, the voices do not belong to my children. Once again I know I must be dreaming. I try, but to no avail, to comprehend what I am seeing. Stepping down and over the threshold, I once again enter my grandparents' kitchen. My mother is sitting in Granddad's chair, next to the fire. In her arms, she nurses a baby to her breast. Sweetly, she sings a lullaby, humming when the words are perhaps forgotten. The baby stops intermittently suckling and makes a cooing sound of contentment. My mother smiles down at the baby. Over by the sink unit, my grandmother, with her back to me, appears to have her hands in water. On the drainer is a selection of washed vegetables. The fire is well stoked and the room is much warmer than the one I have just come from. Two young boys sit at the kitchen table. In their hands, they hold colouring pencils and appear to be drawing pictures. I feel so excited, as I recognise the two boys to be none other than my older brothers. They squabble over the crayons and are reprimanded by my grandmother.

"Come on now you two, keep the noise down. You will disturb your sister while she is feeding."

Both boys look sheepishly towards their grandmother before continuing with their pictures.

"Look, Mummy, do you like my rainbow picture?" It is John who seeks the compliment from our mother.

"Yes, it is beautiful, John."

"I'm drawing a picture of our garden, Mummy. See all the pretty flowers?" It is Douglas's turn to show off his talent.

"Yes, Douglas, your picture is beautiful too."

The two boys are dressed similarly, both wearing short trousers and knee-length socks. Both wear slightly tired, knitted sweaters and I can see the odd darn repair on at least one of each of their sleeves. Their hairstyles are typical of the nineteen forties; short and neat with, I suspect, a small amount of grease to help keep the hair in place. Douglas has inherited our grandmother's auburn hair, whereas John's is more of a mousy colour. The domesticity of the scene I am observing consumes my attention. The innocence of the children, carefree and happy, makes me long for my lost youth. How I wish I could go back to those early years of my childhood and play, once again, with my brothers.

The drawing and colouring activity has consumed the attention of both boys for long enough and they start to become irritable. I watched as Douglas leant over John's work and created a small scribble on his completed picture, he cheekily checked that the adults in the room were not looking in his direction before doing so. In retaliation, John threw his pencil across the table and I watched as it struck his brother on his chin.

"Ouch! That really hurt me."

"I don't care. You have ruined my picture now. Mum, look what Douglas has done to my picture!"

"Come on, boys, stop the fighting. You are upsetting your sister."

Our grandmother quickly tries to intervene in the squabble, but not before Douglas has a chance to call John a freckle face.

"Don't call me that, you know I don't like it."

"That's enough, the both of you," she tells them. "Douglas, you should know better than that. It's not nice calling people names."

"Well, he shouldn't have thrown his pencil at me."

His chin is reddened by the act and he rubs it repeatedly, which makes it even more pronounced.

John, concerned that he would get another telling off, starts a feeble cry.

"Come on, John, stop that silly crying. You know what that say about having freckles."

I knew exactly what she was about to say as I had heard it repeated many times during my childhood. Just like my brothers, I also had my fair share of freckles.

"A face without freckles is like the sky without stars. And anyway, John, you also have freckles of your own."

Looking at both boys, it was clear to see that John's freckles were more noticeable than his brother's, although Douglas did have several small ones across his nose.

A tap at the door startles me, and at the same time ends the feud between the boys.

My grandmother had obviously been expecting the visitor and calls out, "Come on in, Mary, I've got my hands tied at the moment."

The door opens and I can see the caller's familiar face; it is Sister Mary.

"Hello, Megan, how are Ruby and the baby today?"

She doesn't see them straight away. She closes the door and turns around, her face beams as she notices Ruby, sitting in the chair breastfeeding her baby.

I feel slightly amused as, once again, I realise that the baby and myself are one and the same.

"I didn't expect to see you up yet, Ruby. Don't you go doing too much too soon will you?"

I watch as Sister Mary takes off her coat and rolls up her sleeves, as I had seen her do before. She takes out a pair of white elasticised cuffs from her bag and puts them on over her rolled sleeves. Removing the belt from her waist, she then opens her bag and takes out a pristine white folded apron and puts it on. The belt is then returned to her trim waist. The apron bib is fastened to her uniform with two safety pins.

"It's lovely and warm in here. They say it might snow later today." Sister Mary grins at the boys as she makes this statement.

The two boys are excited at the prospect of snow.

"We can try out our new sledge if we get lots of snow, can't we, Mummy?" Douglas looks to our mother for approval.

"We will have to see. Now I think it's time you boys go outside for some fresh air. You have been under Nanny's feet for long enough. Time for the adults to have some time to themselves."

Both boys get down from the table, scraping the chair legs over the floor noisily. The noise startles the baby and she begins to cry, her feed has been momentarily suspended.

"Better get used to that, my little one, boys will be boys and your brothers are no exception when it comes to doing things 'quietly'."

The boys rush towards the door.

"Come on, John, let's play fighting soldiers. We can both be on the same team."

The brothers are friends again.

"You will need to put on coats and hats before you go out."

I watch as Nanny gets these from the cupboard under the stairs. As the boys put on their attire, she takes out a tin from the dresser cupboard and two excited boys each take a piece of what looks like a fruit bread.

"That will keep you going till lunchtime. Now go and find Granddad and see if he has any chores for you to do before you play your game."

My mother calls out to them, just as the door is about to close, "Douglas, make sure you look after your brother. Don't let him out of your sight."

"I will, Mum, don't worry."

Both boys are excited and eager to get outside to play. In their haste, they let the door bang shut and the baby reacts with a cry.

"Oh dear, what am I going to do with those boys? Shush, little one, they are gone now."

I watch my mother as she successfully soothes her baby once again and the breastfeeding continues.

Sister Mary moves closer to her patients, tucking in the chairs as she passes the table.

"Now let me see you both. How are you feeling, Ruby?"

"I feel so much better having had the blood transfusion. I just couldn't wait to get home. The hospital is so busy, I think they were glad to let me go."

Sister Mary smiles as she looks down on the contented baby.

"She is beautiful, Ruby. I am so glad everything is OK. I will never be able to apologise enough for not being with you that night."

Sister Mary takes a handkerchief from her pocket. She blows her nose and I believe it's an excuse to wipe away a tear. My grandmother is quickly at her side.

"You cannot blame yourself, Mary. We both know you couldn't have got through to us that night, with the air raid. It was just unfortunate timing. We managed alright didn't we, Ruby, my love?"

"Yes, but she could have died too." Sister Mary cannot control herself anymore and cries openly.

My grandmother is by her side immediately and offers her comfort.

"We must put it behind us. I thank God that we are all safe now. Things could have been so much worse."

I am stunned at what was being spoken about. Why am I being witness to all this information? From their conversation, I can only surmise that the nurse has been referring to the death of a second baby.

Grandmother continues to offer comfort and reassurance to Sister Mary.

"If you had been there, I don't believe that things would have been any different, the little one was so small and weak. I did everything I could, but she would not respond."

If the baby in my mother's arms is me then I know, for certain, that I must have been one of the twins!

The baby appears to have finished its feed. She lies sleeping peacefully, satisfied with her tummy filled with milk.

"If she has finished her feed, can I have a cuddle with her?" Sister Mary takes the sleeping baby from her mother. Retrieving a square of muslin from the table, she first places it over her shoulder. "She is much smaller than John and Douglas, but then again, you went full term with both of them.

I remember delivering both of them here, at home. More women are opting to have their babies in hospital now. Perhaps next time I should encourage you to do the same."

"I don't think that will be necessary, Sister, no more babies for me. I have two handsome boys, and now a beautiful daughter. I think that's enough for one family, don't you?"

For a few seconds, Sister Mary is quiet, absorbed in her thoughts. From a cuddle held position, she lifts the baby upright.

"I had better keep her upwards on my shoulder as she has just finished a feed."

The whole scenario before me seems so surreal. Seeing myself as a baby, the whole thing is quite obscure. I accept that I must be dreaming, but it still seems so real.

Nanny moves across the room to take the baby from Sister Mary.

"I expect you want to check on Ruby now."

"I could quite easily sit here all day, cuddling your baby, but I guess I had better get on. Shall we go upstairs, Ruby?"

When they have left the kitchen, Nanny cradles the baby in her arms. With one arm holding the baby, she uses her free hand to plump the seat cushion and sits down in Granddad's chair. Smiling to herself, she looks admiringly at the baby and plants little soft kisses on her forehead.

"It's not going to be easy getting through this horrible war, my sweetheart, but I will take the greatest care of you and your family and no matter what the future holds, I will always love you. I am so sorry that I lost your little sister."

How strange to listen to her speaking these words. My beloved nanny had obviously been badly affected by this traumatic experience.

Unbeknown to me, she would continue to blame herself and suffer remorse for the rest of her life.

It's not long before Sister Mary and my mother return to the warmth of the kitchen. Sister Mary turns her attention to the baby.

"Any concerns with the baby, Ruby?" she asks.

"None at all, she is such a good baby, just feeds and sleeps."

"Don't forget your extra rations now. I have a list of entitlements for you both. We've got to look after our war mums and their babies. Remember, you are doing your part by helping the country. Sadly, we are losing a lot of our men to this terrible war. By the way, I forgot to ask after Daniel, did he get off alright?"

"Yes, thank you, his regiment moved out yesterday. He suspected they were being sent to North Africa but won't be told until this evening. He was so happy to see his new daughter before he left and to know that I was going to be alright. The boys are missing him already!"

"I will remember him in my prayers. How is Granddad?" This question directed to my grandmother.

"He's fine. There is so much more to do on the estate now that the young men are gone. He works late like they all do, then comes home to continue his home guard duties. This bloody war."

I don't ever recall my grandmother swearing, but in these circumstances, I can fully appreciate her sentiments.

"I must be getting on. I'm on nit nurse duty today at the school this afternoon."

The ladies in the room all giggle at that statement. Memories of the nit nurse visiting our school when I was young came flooding back. I recall the nurse in her navy colour uniform. She used a knitting needle, which was kept in a jam jar of disinfectant. The teachers would usher us all into a long queue where we would wait in turn for the nurse to search through our hair with the needle. I inhale as I remember the strong smell of the disinfectant, a smell that I have always been fond of.

"By the way, Mary, if it's alright by you, then Daniel and I would like to name our baby after you, your full name, if that's OK? Rosemary Ann."

This news came as quite a shock to me, as well as Sister Mary, and I am completely stunned. I had never known that I had been named after anyone. Baptised Rosemary Ann as a baby, I had chosen to call myself Ann in my late teens. I had thought it simpler and more grown-up.

Sister Mary was obviously delighted, her rosy face beamed. Once again, she took a handkerchief from her pocket to dab at her moist eyes.

"I am overwhelmed, I don't know what to say. I feel so honoured. Thank you, Ruby."

Observing the three women as they said their goodbyes, I realised how close a relationship they had shared. Sister Mary removed her apron and put on her coat and hat. As my grandmother opened the door for her, in preparation for her departure, I could see that snowflakes had started to fall. Sister Mary stepped outside and gave a little shiver.

"Already starting to snow, keep warm, won't you."

As she passed by the window, she gave a little wave.

The room was very quiet. My grandmother turned her attention to her daughter.

"Time for you both to have a rest now."

Following my grandmother's instructions, my mother once again turned to climb the stairs, this time carrying a sleeping baby in her arms. As she passed by her mother, she stopped and gave her a kiss.

"I love you, Mum."

"And I love you too, both of you."

My grandmother returned to the sink and tidied up the washed crockery. She then removed her apron and went to the cupboard, taking out a pair of shoes and a coat. I watched her as she sat down to tie her shoelaces, rubbing her back as she stood up again. The green tweed full-length coat was a little worn but it fitted perfectly, accentuating her tiny frame. On her head, she pinned a small black felt hat, tucking in her wavy auburn hair and peering into a small mirror as she did so. From the same cupboard, under the stairs, she took out a wicker basket. From the basket, she took out a selection of ration books and began to flick through them. I noticed the different array of coloured books and remembered that my mother had once told me that the colours represented rations for different age groups. There was buff for adults and green for pregnant and nursing mums and included children under five years of age. The blue book was for children over five. Realizing that she would probably need them all, she replaced them in her basket. Opening one of the drawers in the dresser, she took out a small zipped purse which she opened to check on its contents. Moving to the fireplace, she stood on tiptoe and reached for the Toby jug that stood on the mantle shelf, removing a paper note which she added to her purse. Quietly, she lifted the latch and went outside, closing the door behind her.

As she passed by the window, she turned and briefly looked in, causing me to take a step back. She was smiling, and I felt sure her smile was directed at me. Could she really see me or know that I was there? The strangest things can occur in dreams.

It was now eerily quiet, save for the ticking grandfather clock in the corner of the room. With the fire still burning in the grate, the room felt cosy and warm. I realised I had not moved from the doorway, from where I had entered and had watched as the domestic scene unfolded.

My mind is confused as I try to understand why I can see and hear, so clearly, my relatives from the past. My body feels extremely weary and I have a strong desire to rest now and feel the need to lay down. Taking the slightly worn patchwork cushion from Granddad's chair, I place it on the small multi-coloured rag rug in front of the fireplace. No longer able to physically stand, I lower myself to the floor. Curling up my legs into a fetal position, I rock gently back and forth until I fall asleep like a baby.

"Wake up, Ann. What are you doing on the floor? You silly girl, it's freezing in here."

"Leave me alone, I'm so cosy by the fire."

I am vaguely aware that a pair of strong arms lift me off the floor until I am consumed in pain and have to cry out.

"Sorry, my love, I cannot leave you on the kitchen floor. You feel so cold."

Is it a reaction to being told that I am cold that causes me to instigate a shiver?

"You promised me you would ring the bell if you needed anything," Jamie's voice sounds angry and I respond to it.

"Please, Jamie, don't be angry with me. I just wanted the kids to keep the noise down a bit. They have brought some of their friends back home and it's very late. I could hear them in the kitchen."

No sooner had I spoken these words that I realised I must have been dreaming. There had been no one in the kitchen, at least I don't think so.

"You silly thing, Matt's not coming home tonight. Don't you remember, he was meeting Abbie off the train and then staying overnight with her parents and Lottie and Pete went home after supper." He still sounded angry.

Jamie carried me, it seemed, with ease back to the lounge which has become my sanctuary. Once in bed, he pulled the blankets up and over my shoulders. My body continued to uncontrollably shiver. I could not be sure if I was feeling cold or if it was the shock from my strange, and so real, dreams. Laying down by my side, I nested my head on Jamie's chest. The strong beat of his heart was bounding rapidly in his chest to start and then, as he calmed down, it began to settle into a more regular and relaxed rhythm. The clock chimed for two o'clock. The room was in darkness. Jamie's voice was reduced to a softer tone as he began to question my sanity.

"Were you having one of those bad dreams again?"

I don't recall as having ever referred to my dreams as being 'bad'. Confusing perhaps, or bizarre, but never bad. Perhaps... I thought that I should keep this one to myself.

"Just a silly dream about the children when they were teenagers. Do you remember when they would come home late on a Saturday night and bring friends in for coffee?"

"That was only yesterday, wasn't it?" he jested. He was obviously beginning to forgive me.

"Come on, my love, let's try and get some more sleep. Are you sure you don't need me to get you anything?"

I knew that he was referring to the bottle of morphine tablets sitting on the side table.

"No thanks. I think I will be alright till morning."

It was not long before I could tell that Jamie had fallen asleep. Unable to switch off like he could, I pondered on the events that my dream had divulged. Why is it so important for me to know what may or may not have happened when I was born? Is it the morphine that makes me have these dreams or is there something deep within my subconscious that is trying to find a way through?

The other alternative answer is that I am seeing ghosts. Whatever it is, I believe it is keeping me sane, as opposed to Jamie's concerns that I may be going insane. The last scan I had been given had shown up small irregularities in my brain tissue. Perhaps this was the cause?

Tomorrow, I decided, I would speak openly with John, knowing it will most definitely be the last time I will see him.

Feeling warmer now, and safe with Jamie beside me, I breathe slowly through the irregular bouts of pain that seem to come and go. I know that if I remain still, the pain is more manageable and eventually I am able to succumb to sleep.

"Happy birthday, Ann."

Rubbing my eyes to clear away the sleepy dust, the cheeky smile of Jamie can be clearly seen peering at me.

"Thank you, love. What time is it?" I ask simultaneously as I turn towards the clock.

"Nearly seven. Did you sleep OK after your escapade last night?"

"I'm sorry, Jamie, I guess I was just a little confused."

"Do you want to talk about it?"

The opportunity to talk about my dreams to Jamie is overwhelming but I am afraid he will not take me seriously. He can tell from my slow response that I am in two minds as to whether to share my experience with him.

"Come on, Ann, I know it's causing you concern. Maybe Jill can ask the doctor for a different drug to try? There must be alternatives to morphine."

That's it, my mind is made up and I decide not to tell him about the peculiar, yet so real, dream of last night.

"No that's OK, I don't want to change the morphine because it really helps me when the pain is bad." I know I am probably addicted and would rather live with the side effects than be without it.

It was time for the first walk of the day, to the bathroom. Jamie assists me to a sitting position. With his help, I manage to stand awkwardly upright; a shooting pain in my spine and I fall back onto the bed. Jamie's strong arms are quickly there to support me.

"I'm sorry, Jamie, I don't think I can do it today." I was concerned that I had probably overdone it earlier when, without remembering, I had managed to walk to the kitchen.

"Don't worry, Ann. I think it might be time to use the wheelchair. I'll fetch it from the study."

When Jill suggested that I might like to have a wheelchair, I had protested. Jamie, however, had kept it in his study and away from my view. Inwardly, I knew that I would need it at some time in the future but did not expect that some time would come this soon.

"Yes, OK, I think it's for the best."

Jamie wheeled the chair to my side. On its seat, I noticed a newly worked patchwork cushion. It was not something I had seen before. On closer inspection, I could recognise some of the materials that had been used.

"Where did the cushion come from?"

"Lottie made it with scraps of material from your work basket. It was going to be a Christmas present for you, but she thought you would like to use it in this chair. It was to be a surprise because she knew how you felt about using a wheelchair."

"It's beautiful. Look, it has pieces of her bridesmaids' material."

There were other pieces I recognised; a selection of floral print material which had been used by my mother to make summer dresses for herself, and also for Lottie. Memories came flooding back of my mother sitting at her sewing machine and the ease in which she could work the machine stitching. My mother was able to turn any simple piece of material into a respectable copy of a modern garment. Sadly, this was not one of her talents that I had shared.

"Let's try it out for comfort."

Stabilising the breaks, Jamie helped me into the wheelchair.

"It's a shame to sit on it but if Lottie made it for me then I would love to use it."

It certainly took my mind off the thought of using the wheelchair. Clever and thoughtful Lottie, I think to myself. As I am wheeled to the bathroom, I remember another slightly faded patchwork cushion that I had seen recently, was this yet another coincidence?

Ablutions completed, and with clean linen on my bed, I felt more comfortable. The simple task, however, always takes its toll on me and I feel exhausted. With a breakfast tray on my lap, I attempt to eat a little bread and banana. The bread sticks in my throat and the fruit is tasteless. A few sips of energy drink is all I can manage. My body is wasting fast now and I know I cannot go on for much longer.

"Is that all you can manage to eat?" Jamie looks at the untouched tray and studies me closely. I know he is worried and I try to lighten his mood.

"I am saving myself for the cake later."

I must wait another hour for Jill to arrive. Resting back on my pillow, I close my eyes but open them periodically to check the time on the clock, such is my eagerness for the next dose of morphine. Resting back on my pillow, I listen as Jamie completes a few domestic chores before he retires to the study. The bell is placed on the small side table and in easy reach. Not that I need it when he is downstairs, for I can shout to him from here.

"Don't you dare try and move without ringing that bell first!" Jamie's voice is firm but he smiles at me with a twinkle in his eye.

"I wouldn't dare," I reply.

The truth of the matter is that I knew I couldn't get up on my own even if I tried.

The pain is getting worse and I am not sure that I can wait for Jill much longer. Perhaps I should take a tablet now rather than wait for the quicker pain relief injection.

A knock at the door, followed by a second one, reminds me that I do not expect Jill this morning. She would always knock the door but then let herself in. I hear Jamie walking towards the door. It had been opened and Jamie's voice could be heard greeting the caller. The door was then closed and I could hear the pair of them talking in the hallway. They seem to stay there for quite some time and I become irritable. Nothing, however, prepares me for the shock I have when they finally enter the lounge.

The woman in uniform, standing in front of me, is of a similar age to me. Strangely, her appearance is not dissimilar to my own or at least the one I had before I became ill. Naturally, she has a full head of hair, darker than mine had been. Her voice, however, was uncanny, so similar to that of my mother that if I had closed my eyes I would have believed that I was talking to her.

"Hello, Ann. Can I call you by your first name?" Smiling, she takes a step forward and offers her hand to shake mine. Our eyes scrutinize each other and as our hands touch, I am sure she experiences the same feelings as I, of déjà vu.

"I'm Ruth."

In her hand, she held a single red rose.

"A little bird told me it is your birthday today." Offering me the gift of the flower, she wished me a happy day.

She obviously doesn't notice any likeness between the two of us as I do, why should she, when my appearance is so changed from what it was.

"That is so kind of you. I am very pleased to meet you, Ruth."

"Funny," Ruth continues, "I have a strange feeling we might have met before. Jill tells me that you are also a nurse. Perhaps we have met at a nursing conference or study day?"

Changing the subject, she goes on to explain that she has my care plan and knows all about me. Sitting down in the chair opposite me, she takes out the brown medical folder from her bag. I could see there were three others in the bag as well as mine.

"Jill has told me all about you. She said I had to give you the very best attention and that you were a special lady. I like to think all my patients are special though," she adds with a genuine friendly smile.

There is something warming about her mannerisms and I take to her instantly. Ruth has obviously been well informed of my needs. She concludes her examination of me and administers my injections. One for pain and the other for nausea. With her jobs completed, she brings her paperwork and sits down next to me. Quietly, she sits and fills in the relevant boxes on the paper. How strange, I think to myself, that she should give me a rose, and I study her more closely. How could she know that roses, like my grandmother, were my favourite flowers?

"Tell me about yourself, Ruth." I realise that I may have spoken without thinking. "I hope you won't think I am being nosey but you do seem so familiar." I know I have nothing to lose so continue to ask my questions.

"Not a lot to tell," she starts. "I have lived in London most of my life. Nursing is the only job I have ever done. I trained at St Thomas in London."

"What brings you to this part of the country, Ruth?" I continue searching for more information.

"My parents came from Sussex and spoke very affectionately about this area in particular. My father was a vicar here before the war. They moved to London when the war was over. So much was needed to be done there. Not just rebuilding houses but people's lives also."

"And are your parents still alive?"

"No, sadly they were killed in a car accident a long time ago. I was only ten years old at the time."

"I am so sorry. I should not be asking you these questions."

Now I do feel guilty, for being nosey, and sorry for her loss.

"It's OK. I don't mind talking about it," she continues.

"Strange though, it only seems like yesterday that I was told of the news. I remember it so well."

Ruth put down her paperwork and places her pen in the top pocket of her uniform. She folds her hands together on her lap.

"I went to live with my mother's sister, Auntie Irene. She became my second mum. In fact, I used to call her this before my parents died as I had spent as much of my time with her as I did with them."

Ruth became quiet as if pondering on the past.

Again I apologised for asking so many questions.

"That's OK, Ann. It was all a long time ago. I am enjoying talking to you. For some reason I cannot explain, you seem familiar to me. Chatting to you comes easily."

Ruth seemed more relaxed. She went on to tell me about her husband who worked in general practice. Her eldest son, who has followed in his father's footsteps and now, works in the paediatric department in their local hospital. Her younger son had joined the Royal Air Force and worked as a mechanic. She went on to explain that her job here was just for a three-month secondment from her hospital in London.

"You have an excellent nurse-led palliative care team here. The opportunity became available, for someone to spend some time here and learn about how it all works. I have worked in palliative care for some years but we are a little behind when it comes to nurse-led care in the community. I am hoping to take back some ideas."

The morphine has done its job. The pain is much less. With the good comes the bad and I feel very drowsy. A sensitive, caring, nurse by the name of Ruth realises her patient is struggling to stay awake.

"I have been talking too much. It's time I left you to rest."

Lifting up my thin, bony hand, to object to her leaving, she gently places it in her own. With my other hand, I cover hers.

"It's been such a pleasure meeting you, Ann. Now, before I go, can I do anything else for you? Of course, I will be back this evening to settle you for the night but just like Jill, you can call me earlier if you need me."

I really don't want her to leave. It is with reluctance that I let go of her hand. I do not understand my feelings towards her. Confused and at the same time agitated, I make attempts to keep her there with my objections, which now border on mutterings, no longer being decipherable. It is only a short time before I succumb to sleep and she is gone.

In my dream, he visits me again, the tall man in a black coat and hat. He stands at the bottom of my bed and bows his head. Slowly, he moves to my side and bends over me. I am determined to look into his face. A sallow drawn face stares back at me. Not an unkind one, but one of pitiful sadness. His dark eyes appear to plead with me. A voice speaks gently to me.

"Forgive me, forgive me," the words repeated over and over again.

Reaching out with my hand, I try to touch him. My hand is suspended in the air. There is no form to feel, just a cool sensation that flows through my fingers and down my arm. The dark shadow is motionless.

"Why are you so sad, why do you need forgiveness?"

He withdraws from my side and moves slowly backwards and as he reaches the wall, he disappears through it.

"Don't go, don't leave me," I plead. Tears of sadness fill my eyes and I cannot control my sobbing.

Jamie is working in the study when my crying disturbs him.

"What is it, Ann? I am here. I'm not going anywhere. Have you been dreaming again?"

Jamie helps me to sit up and protectively cradles me in his arms and all this while I continue to sob.

"Oh, Jamie, I know you won't believe me but he was here again. The tall man in the black coat, but this time, I spoke to him."

"Shh! My love, it was just a dream."

"No. He was definitely here and he looked so sad that he made me cry. He wants forgiveness but I don't know what from."

Jamie continued to try and console me with gentle restraint but I would have none of it; fighting him off with every bit of strength I could muster and begging him to listen to me.

"OK," he said, letting go of me, "calm down and tell me what it is you thought you saw."

With nothing to lose, I told him about the apparition of the man and of the words he had spoken to me. For a few moments, Jamie did not respond. He appeared to be in deep thought. Not wanting to cause me any more distress, he told me that he believed me and that together we would work it out.

He gently soothed my head with his warm hand and I eventually succumbed to deeper and more peaceful sleep.

It was lunchtime when I awoke. The chimes on the clock had just struck twelve-thirty. I could hear someone in the kitchen preparing food. Sighing, I adjusted my position to be more comfortable.

Jamie must have heard me and within seconds was by my side.

"Did you have a good sleep, love?"

"Yes, thank you."

"I was just going to have a bite of lunch, fancy joining me?"

I saw that he was already nibbling at what looked like a stick of celery.

"Not just yet, thanks. I need to wake up a bit more first. I slept so soundly."

Jamie returned to the kitchen and came back carrying a tray of food.

"I will just eat my soup and sandwiches and give you some time to come to. Then I will bring you some soup."

With his tray on his lap, I watched him as he tasted the soup.

"Delicious, but very hot!"

Replacing the spoon on the tray he then picked up the first of his sandwiches and devoured it. Just the sight and smell of the food made me feel nauseous. Not wanting him to know how I was feeling, I turned my gaze to the clock on the mantelpiece, to take my mind off the food.

Having come to, and now feeling more awake, I began to remember the dream I had had. Feeling in a calmer mood, I asked Jamie what he thought of the new nurse Ruth.

"She seems very nice. Reminds me a little of you in her mannerisms."

In those few words, he had hit the nail on the head and I was relieved to hear him say this.

"I thought we had met somewhere before and so did she," I continued to explain, "she seemed so familiar. I can't explain why but I would like her to meet John."

"She won't be able to do that, Ann. Don't forget, he leaves this afternoon for Devon so won't be staying for very long this afternoon."

"Yes, I had forgotten. Never mind."

After I had thought more logically about it, I realised it didn't really matter anyway. The peculiar things that have occurred, both before and during (and exacerbated by) my illness, had left me convinced that someone had prepared me for the meeting with Ruth. Although I could hardly believe it myself, the only explanation was that she must be my twin sister. What had taken place at the time of our birth, I would probably never know. This did not matter anymore. This was something only I needed to know about and I would take these newfound revelations to my grave.

I watched again as Jamie devoured his soup and the second of the two sandwiches, which had been stuffed full with cold meat and salad. Even for him, the thickness of the sandwich was too much to fit his mouth and I smiled as some of the contents fell back onto the plate and a small amount fell onto the front of his shirt.

"Oh, dear, one more shirt for the wash."

When he had finished, he went back to the kitchen and within a few minutes returned carrying a tray of food for me. Under his watchful eye, I managed to eat a few spoonfuls of warm soup. If he hadn't have told me that it was of a chicken variety, I would not have known. Two peeled grapes completed my meal and I soon began to feel nauseous again.

"I'm sorry, Jamie, I feel sick."

Jamie retrieved a disposable cardboard bowl that was kept under the table, only 'just' in time. With both hands clutching my stomach, where the pain became worse as I wretched, I spewed the contents of my just eaten lunch back into the bowl. Supporting my head and shoulders with one arm, Jamie held the bowl close to my mouth.

"It's OK, my love, I'm here."

Exhausted, I lay back on the pillow and Jamie took a tissue from the box and wiped my mouth.

"Feeling better?"

"Thank you. I'm sorry about that."

"Don't you worry, I won't tell Pete that you didn't like his chicken soup."

Typical of Jamie, to make light of the situation and in doing so make me smile.

After he had cleaned up, Jamie sat down in the chair next to me and soothed my brow. The warmth and tenderness of his hand was comforting and I relaxed. Sitting by my side, we talked about the children and the arrangements for Christmas. We had discussed this many times over the last few weeks; I was adamant that it had to be special and that my final days were not going to be wasted on sadness.

In my heart, I am uncertain if I will indeed see Christmas day.

During my melancholic days, I had wondered if I was being fair to my family by wanting to see another Christmas. What would happen if I were to die on Christmas day itself? How would everyone cope with it? Am I being selfish?

"Penny for your thoughts," Jamie was studying me.

"I was just thinking, perhaps we had better get a move on before everyone arrives," I lied.

With an exerted, painful, effort, I let Jamie take me to the bathroom in the wheelchair. I couldn't even manage a small wee. Replacing one dry sanitary pad for a fresh one, I knew that I must be very dehydrated. My belly looked swollen and felt solid to the touch. With a warm cloth, I tried to wash my face and, as I leant over the basin, I saw my reflection staring back at me from the vanity mirror. I looked so much older than my years! My face was thin and bony and my skin was sallow and jaundiced, with dark sunken eyes. Under my breath, I muttered to myself.

"Dear God, let it be soon."

Lottie and Pete were the first to arrive, carrying more boxes of food. In her hands, Lottie was carrying a birthday cake.

"Happy birthday, Mum," she presented the cake with a kiss.

"You are both so kind to me, and what a beautiful cake." The cake was pink and covered with tiny edible roses.

"Pete's masterpiece I think," Jamie added.

Everyone went through to the kitchen except for Lottie.

"Mum, I need to talk to you but I am finding it difficult," Lottie was struggling with her words.

"Come here, Lottie and sit with me," I smile because I know what she is about to say and I want her to know that everything will be just fine. "I'm going to tell you something first, Lottie. When you become a parent yourself, you will have a second sense about the welfare of your children and quite often, you will know certain things about them before they do themselves."

Lottie hugs me.

"You know, don't you, that Pete and I are expecting a baby? I didn't know whether to tell you or not, it just seems so cruel that you will not be here to see your first grandchild."

Her eyes filled with tears and I knew that I had to remain strong.

"Lottie, I may not be visible to you when I am gone but you must understand that I will still be here. Little things like memories. Have you forgotten?"

Taking a tissue to wipe away her sadness, I remind her of my grandmother's wisdom and the poem she would always recite.

"I am so happy for you both and I beg of you to be happy too. Now go and tell Granddad the news and tell him I said to put some champagne on ice. This is the best birthday news anyone could have been given! Also, thank you for the perfect patchwork cushion for my chair."

That's it, no more tears. No more dreams. It's no longer about me! I will be strong and happy for my last remaining days.

What an afternoon we had. Mathew and Abbie arrived, arms laden with flowers. It was lovely just to listen to the youngsters chattering. Lottie told them the news of her pregnancy. Shortly after this, Jill arrived. Champagne was opened and each had a glass to celebrate the news. I dipped a

149

finger in a glass and sucked the sour taste from it and pretended that it was delicious.

"Shouldn't really drink this with medication," I joked.

With the arrival of my brother John and his wife Jean, another bottle of champagne was opened. John had a sip to celebrate but declined to drink any more as he was shortly to drive on to Devon. Pete, once again, had prepared the food; small, bite-size, finger food was handed around to everyone. Lastly, the cake was cut for everyone to enjoy. I had requested that the birthday song was not sung, as everyone had already wished me a happy day and I was enjoying the day immensely.

Jamie took John to his study. He had some gifts for the twins that Lottie had chosen. Jean was excited about the news of Lottie's forthcoming event and was offering lots of advice to the parents to be. Jill came and sat with me and we had a few precious minutes alone together.

"I know I'm not on duty, but I just want to check you're OK. You look tired, Ann, how is the pain?"

"I'm OK, thanks. All of this excitement takes my mind off the pain. By the way, Ruth was lovely this morning. Not as lovely as you, of course," I added quickly with a smile.

"I'm glad you liked her, Ann. She interviewed well and I'm getting a lot of positive feedback from our patients. She will be back this evening and then I will see you tomorrow."

Jill got to her feet and made to leave.

"You're not leaving so soon?"

"Yes, I'm afraid I must. There are still lots to do before the family descend on me for the holidays."

She bends over me and kisses my cheek, squeezing my hand gently at the same time.

"I love you, Ann. Enjoy the rest of the day."

Then she whispers in my ear the words that she knew I needed to hear, "don't worry, I will look after Lottie for you and see that she is OK."

We have known each other for so long that words have not always been necessary, but this time, I was truly grateful.

"Thank you, Jill. You have been the best friend anyone could have asked for."

The children subtly move away to the kitchen when it is time for me to say goodbye to my brother. We hold each other closely. When he pulls back, I notice his tears.

"Come on, John, none of that now. We will see each other again you know, I am convinced of that."

It is strange that the one who is dying must be the one to support those that will be left behind. I know that I can do this because I am stronger now, influenced possibly by the morphine. I also think my dreams and apparitions have helped me in preparing for my death.

"Not on this earth perhaps," I continue, "but I am in no doubt that it will be a beautiful place. Take care of your family and send them my love."

The preparation for the departure of John and Jean is a lingering one. First, in the hallway and then in the drive, as they buckle up for their journey to Devon. Unable to witness them driving away, I listen to the muffled sounds of chatter and then the engine sound of the car pulling away down the drive.

"God bless you, John."

Somewhere during the course of the afternoon, Pete had offered accommodation for Mathew and Abbie. He had suggested it was an opportunity for them to spend some time together and to catch up. No doubt they would spend the evening playing board games and drinking beer. Taking each child simultaneously by their hands, I thanked them for making it such a lovely day.

"Enjoy yourselves tonight, but don't keep Lottie up too late," I hastened to add, in a jovial tone of voice.

With the children gone, the house resumed its quiet atmosphere.

Sighing softly to myself, I realise that I feel quite relaxed and inwardly happy. Jamie switches on the Christmas lights before leaving me to go and tidy the kitchen.

Just like it always does this time of year, the evening begins to draw in early. It is only five o'clock. The lights sparkle once again, creating a magical scene. They flicker through the shadows in the darkest corners of the room. It is truly mystical and fills me with a sense of spiritual wellbeing. Closing my eyes in meditation helps me to maintain the relaxation that I am enjoying. The power of mind over body feels stronger and the pain is drawn away from me. Never have I experienced such control. My body is limp and I feel that at any time I will float away.

"Ann, can I get you anything," a voice calling from the kitchen.

And I am suddenly brought back from a state that I can only believe is euphoria.

Jamie had finished the chores. It's probably a good thing I can't see inside the kitchen. Before I became too ill to look after the house, I had been very house-proud and had high standards which I expected everyone else to observe. Jamie returned from the kitchen looking very pleased with himself and I knew it was because of the prospects of becoming a grandfather.

"Time for us now."

"Yes, it is."

I have always enjoyed the dark winter evenings, cuddled up with Jamie in front of the television, or just listening to music. My eyes follow Jamie as he moves about the room. I wonder how much he will miss me when I am no longer around.

"Shall I put on some music?"

Our record selection is vast and he chooses one of my favourite classical records, before joining me on the bed. With my head resting on his lap, we discuss the events of the day. He was excited with the news of Lottie's pregnancy and promised me he would take exceptional care of both our children. He is the second person today to reassure me that our children would be alright when I am no longer around. Gently, he strokes my head as we become silent and listen to music.

It is only when his hand is still that I realise he has fallen asleep. Looking up into his face, I admire his slightly rugged good looks. Not as young anymore, but still attractive to me and with a full head of hair, albeit silver-grey in colour. What does he see in me, I wonder? In my younger years, he thought me attractive but I know I am not a pretty site anymore.

"Not long now, Jamie," I whisper to myself. "I have loved you more than you could ever know. You have been a wonderful husband, friend and father. No one could have asked for any more. When I am gone, you will move on because that is my wish for you. You will be sad for a while but don't let your sadness linger for too long. I am ready to go now."

Taking his hand in mine, I hold it like a precious jewel. Not wanting to disturb this tranquillity, I say my prayers quietly to myself.

The clock ticks rhythmically and I move my head to check on the time. It is nearly seven twenty-five. I know the chime on the half-hour will wake Jamie from his sleep. I watch as time moves on and the hands of the clock get ready to pounce, but it does not happen. The large hand has moved past the half-hour without its regular chime. This clock has been like a good friend to me and now it chooses to remain quiet while Jamie sleeps on.

Eight o'clock passes, as does the half-hour, and still, the clock remains quiet, except for its gentle ticking sounds. At nine o'clock, it springs back into life and Jamie stirs.

"Oh dear, I must have dropped off, is that the time? The nurse will be here soon."

As if on cue, Ruth arrived for my evening visit. Jamie excused himself and headed back to his study.

"Hello again, Ann and how are you this evening? I wasn't sure if your guests would have left yet."

"I am quite relaxed this evening, thank you. Everyone left quite early so I was enjoying some time with Jamie, but I am very pleased to see you again."

I studied Ruth some more as she took her instruments from her bag. I wondered if I should say something to her about my intuitions but decided not to.

"A funny thing happened to me today, couldn't quite believe it, such a coincidence." She was preparing my injection as she was talking to me. "Better concentrate on this first though and then I can chat."

The routine procedures completed, and the injection given, Ruth sat down to complete the paperwork. I was eager to hear what she had to say about what had happened that day that had been coincidental. After all, I was quite an expert in coincidences now.

"Ann, would you like me to leave, or shall I stay a while and chat? You are my last patient this evening so I'm in no hurry to leave. It's not the same going back to a room on your own, as it is going home."

I had forgotten for a while that she was away from her home and family.

"Please stay for a chat. Can I get Jamie to get you a cup of tea or coffee or something?"

"That's very kind but no, I am fine, thank you."

Ruth makes me feel very comfortable in her presence and it feels as if I have known her for a longer time than the one day.

"After I left you this morning, I went to the Priory to see my second patient of the day. I couldn't believe my eyes when I saw her. My patient was none other than my nurse tutor from London, who was responsible for me becoming a nurse. Between you and me, I would have given up my training if Miss Thorne hadn't taken me under her wing. She was very kind to me and even visited Auntie Irene to tell her how sad it would be if I were to give up my career in nursing. That in itself was a coincidence because it turned out that Miss Thorne also knew my parents but was surprised that they had a child. Of course, she is an elderly lady now but I still recognised her as soon as I went in. I had seen her name on my list but didn't put two and two together."

I was intrigued to learn more. Could this possibly be the same lady that Jill had mentioned to me the day before?

Ruth continued with her story, stopping to ask me the occasional question.

"I wondered if you knew of her, Ann, as she lived in this village before and during the war years and only moved to London when the war was over. Thinking about it, you probably wouldn't because we are of a similar age and would have been babies during the war."

"Did this lady recognise you, Ruth?"

"Surprisingly, yes. Sister Margaret had told me not to expect much in the way of communication, as she was confused at times, but as soon as she saw me, she said that she recognised me. The interesting thing was that she called me Rosemary and said that I had been named after her. I didn't like to correct her for fear of upsetting her. She seemed genuinely happy to see me."

A shiver ran down my spine as I suddenly realised that the lady in question must be none other than Sister Mary. I remembered that her full name was Rosemary Ann and that I had been named after her.

"If I'm not asking too much of you, can you divulge the name that is written on her notes?"

"I don't see why not. Let me have a look as I have her notes with me in my bag."

Before Ruth could confirm her patient's full name, I had already interrupted her and spoken the name of Rosemary Ann. How could I tell Ruth that I only knew of this lady from the strange dreams I had been having?

"I think I might have been named after this lady."

Ruth looked at my notes again and smiled as she saw that I did indeed share the same name. I went on to explain how I had chosen to shorten my name and call myself Ann. Ruth was as excited as I was.

"Well, isn't that another coincidence," she exclaimed.

"Was Miss Thorne able to say anything else?"

I knew that I was expecting too much of Ruth by continuing to ask questions but I was desperate to find out more information and try to piece together the puzzle that was laid before me. She did not disappoint and continued with her story.

"She seemed genuinely happy to see me and remembered that she had taught me in London. After I had administered her medication, she went quiet and started to cry. She was asking to see someone named Ruby. I asked Sister Margaret who Ruby was and she told me that Ruby had been a friend to her and also the Priory, for many years but had sadly passed away. She told me that Ruby had been particularly friendly towards Miss Thorn and would spend a lot of time with her. When she died, Miss Thorn was never the same again and had missed her friend very much."

I could not absorb any more information as I was beginning to feel very tired. The pieces of puzzle were coming together and my dreams were beginning to make more sense. Ruth could see I was struggling to keep my eyes open and made ready to leave me.

"It's been lovely meeting you, Ann. I won't be here tomorrow as Jill is back. I would, however, love to visit again if you are up to it?"

"Oh yes, please. I would be delighted to see you when you have time to drop in." Inwardly, I knew that the chances of meeting again were very slim. My time was getting very close now.

We hugged each other and I believe we both felt a bond and a special sense of kindred spirit between us. I knew more than she did and I would have to decide as to whether I would share this knowledge with her or keep it to myself.

Jamie helped Ruth on with her coat and led her to the door.

It was getting late and Jamie looked tired. It had been an eventful day in one way or another.

"Please sleep in your bed tonight Jamie. I will be fine on my own."

"Why can't I stay here with you? I am perfectly comfortable you know."

To be honest, I wanted to be alone with my thoughts but could not let Jamie know this.

"It has been a wonderful day and an exhausting one. I will be asleep as soon as you leave the room and I don't have the strength to get up on my own."

"Are you sure there's nothing I can get you?"

"Nothing, thanks."

It is a struggle to keep my eyes open anymore. As was the usual, every night that I had spent with Jamie, I felt his warm lips on mine as he wished me a good night.

"I love you, my darling, sleep well."

"And I you, with all my heart."

Determined to sleep well, I decided to take some extra pain relief medication. With a lot of difficulty, I managed to open the bottle of liquid. Clumsily, I knocked the measuring cup which fell quietly onto the carpeted floor. Bringing the bottle to my lips, I sipped a calculated amount of the liquid. Swallowing was becoming increasingly difficult. A small amount trickled down my chin. Replacing the lid, I placed the bottle on the table that was conveniently to my side.

The room was in near-total darkness. There was no sound. I strained my ears to hear the clock ticking but there was nothing. *Let it rest also,* I thought to myself. It had served me well; always reassuring me by ticking gently to aid my sleep and chiming almost regularly on the hour and the half. Turning my face to the window, where the curtains remained drawn, I could see soft snowflakes falling from the sky. How beautiful it was. I wonder to myself, whether it will be a white Christmas – although I know now that I won't see it.

From across the room, I can hear a voice. It is calling to me.

"Rosemary, it's time now. We have been waiting for you."

Turning my head towards the kitchen, I can see a light. In the foreground of the light, I can visualise my grandmother. She is smiling at me and beckoning to me with her hand.

"We are all here. Don't be frightened, Rosemary."

I am not in the least bit frightened, for I relish this invitation to go to my grandmother. Carefully, I get up from the bed. I walk forward towards the light and into the waiting arms of my grandmother.

# Jamie's Story

# Chapter 1

"I must learn to accept the things I cannot change."

No matter how prepared you think you are, when the time comes, it is still heartbreaking to deal with the death of someone you have shared your life with, someone who became your lover and your best friend. An individual with whom you could share your most intimate of secrets and know that you are safe in doing so. Ann was this woman that I had truly loved so deeply and would miss for the rest of my natural life.

When Ann had first been diagnosed with cancer, I did not know how I was going to cope. How selfish of me to think this way, after all, it wasn't me who had to deal with having this most horrid of diseases. I had been lucky when I too thought that I might have had cancer. It was Ann who was determined to see that I was checked out quickly. She made the appointment for me and was by my side as I underwent the torment of investigations for cancer. She always seemed to know what to say, being supportive, caring and strong. Now roles would be reversed and I would be the one to show my support. I was determined to remain positive in front of Ann, but inside, I was scared. My stomach was tied up in knots and I felt physically sick.

"Don't worry, Ann, you'll be alright, just you wait and see." I had spoken in haste, not thinking before blurting out insensitively. Ann's pale, drawn face just stared back at me, her eyes wide and her mouth open in disbelief.

"How do you know that, Jamie?"

"You are a strong woman, my love. I'm sure you will beat this." There I go again, thoughtless and stupid, spewing out statements without thinking. I felt guilt as Ann covered her face with her hands and burst into tears. I tried to comfort her, taking her into my embrace, tilting her chin so I could look into her tear-stained eyes and more deeply into her whole being. I begged her forgiveness, gently planting soft kisses on every part of her face. This had always worked before when I knew I had been in the wrong. This time, she struggled to be released from my affectionate pose.

"Leave me alone, Jamie, you just don't understand how I am feeling."

Ann grabbed at a cushion from the couch before she slumped down on it. I watched as she rocked herself backwards and forwards, hugging the cushion close to her body.

*That should be me,* I thought to myself. *I am the one she should be hugging right now.* Looking around the room, I sought the box of tissues lying on the coffee table and offered them to her.

"I'm sorry, Ann. I'm just not thinking straight."

I sat down on the couch next to her. *Do I try again to reach out to her,* I thought to myself, *or is it too soon?* I decided not to. Sitting next to her quietly and listening to her crying was not easy, but it gave me time to think about what I wanted to say.

"You know how much I love you, Ann."

"Yes, I know you do – and I love you too."

Ann took a handful of tissues from the box, blew her nose and wiped away her tears. She was trying to find a degree of composure.

"I'm not good when it comes to saying the right thing, Ann. I'm clumsy."

She reached out to me and took my hand. Sniffing back the tears, and then with a little smile, she squeezed it affectionately.

"I know," she said, "I'm sorry too. I guess we both have to try and be more understanding of each other."

How like my Ann; always the one who knew what to say when it mattered.

"I promise you, Ann, that I will do everything I can to help you through this and when I make a mistake, you must promise to tell me because I only want to do what is right for you."

Ann threw her arms around my neck and we clung together. Our tears mingled as we spoke words of love to each other. We each made our apologies, and at the same time, our promises to each other. For the remainder of the afternoon, we lay together on the couch, our bodies entwined and our hearts content. My brave Ann spoke about her cancer. She told me of the possible treatments she may have to endure. I had only a little understanding of cancer, save what I had learnt when I thought that I had the disease myself. What I had learnt had mostly come through Ann's nursing profession and her work in the hospital.

I felt quite numb after she had told me in more detail about the treatments that she might have to endure.

There was no doubt in my mind that I would support her and love her always, no matter what the final outcome might be. In Ann's company, I would do all the things that I had promised her but there were times when I just needed to be away from the disease that was interfering in our lives. In those first few months, following her diagnosis, I tried to lose myself in my work, taking on more than I should have, just to keep my mind busy. In recreation, I would thrash a ball against the wall of the squash court over and over again, swearing under my breath as I did so. My squash partner was my best friend and confidant and was also Jill's husband.

Just as Jill would support Ann, so her husband (and my friend) Neil supported me. Ann would never know the difficulty I had, coming to terms with her cancer. I became a liar to myself, and others, and eventually had to seek help from a cancer support group. It was impossible to expose everything I felt and thought about to Neil, for fear of him discussing our conversations with Jill. Within the support group, I found it easier opening up and talking about my feelings. Everyone within the group was either going through similar experiences, as I was, or had been close to a relative who had sadly passed away from cancer. It was a room where a few people whose lives were consumed with guilt and grief had come together, to share their thoughts and somehow find a way through. After a few meetings, having held back, I began to divulge my innermost feelings, secure in my mind that I would not be judged.

My love for Ann never wavered, not for a single moment and I would never have considered infidelity or desertion. The strongest feelings of love for my Ann would share moments of pity and pride. After the first course of treatment had been completed, she was told that an operation to remove the affected breast was her best option – to stop the cancer cells from spreading. I knew that this was going to be the hardest decision that Ann would have to make. I also knew that my response to her decision would have to contain the most sensitive adjectives that I could think of. It would be another sleepless night when we would lay together in our bed talking about the operation. I was in all honesty, surprised at her reaction when she spoke.

"It's only a breast," she stated, "and if the doctor says it's the best thing for me, then I guess my decision is made."

"You know something, Ann, I'm so very proud of you."

She seemed to be in good spirits and I was taken a bit by surprise.

"I'll still have one breast left, won't I," she jested.

"And I love all of your body, not just your breasts."

"Just as well," she added with a chuckle.

"The most important thing for me is for you to get well, my love."

"Perhaps we should start thinking about booking a holiday next year. I think I might like to use my illness as an excuse for a long convalescence." Ann was being so optimistic and I had no intention of ruining this.

"I did so enjoy our holiday to Cornwall last year. Do you remember the day we found the tunnels and beaches in Ilfracombe?" Ann's face lit up.

"Yes, it was a good find, so relaxing, lying on the beach, resting our eyes after our long walk from the campsite."

Ann had loved the beauty and the history of the segregated Victorian bathing beaches and had tried to imagine how it must have been in those days.

"Do you recall when the little girl walked by us with her mother and commented that she thought we were asleep?"

"Yes, and her mother told her she should be quiet so as not to wake us."

*Happy days,* I thought to myself, as I inwardly prayed that there would be many more to come.

"Where do you think you would like to go for your convalescence, my darling?"

I did not have to wait long for her excited response, "what I really would like to do, if you think we can afford it, is to visit John and Jean in Australia."

"That's a great idea," I happily agreed, "they are always suggesting that we visit them again."

There was now something else for the both of us to think about; planning ahead for a holiday would be the tonic that we both needed, especially Ann.

"Shall I try and call John tomorrow and see when would be convenient for them?"

"Why not."

I did not let on that I had spoken to John in confidence, about my concern for Ann's illness. It might not have been my place to do this but I knew how fond they were of each other and thought that he had a right to know. Ann, however, had decided not to tell him until she had more positive results. Neither of us knew then, that the holiday to Australia would not happen.

# Chapter 2

The day that surgery had taken place, I remained at her side until the anaesthetic had taken effect. Promising to be there when Ann woke, the surgeon determined an approximate time for me to return to the recovery ward. Leaving the hospital and the car in the car park, I walked the busy streets through the town. My pace quickened as I became angry towards the people who seemed to be dawdling as I passed them by, bumping into a few, in eagerness to escape the humdrum of noise made by the carefree shoppers who got in my way. I dodged the traffic, not wanting to stop to cross any road. The last thing I needed was to bump into anyone that I might have known and would have had to stop and make polite conversation with. Following the road out of the town, I found myself climbing the steep hill to reach the church on the top.

St Peter's Church was not one that I had ever visited before; Ann and I having always attended our local village church of St Edmond's. There were two people coming out of the church as I approached, the couple was probably of a similar age to Ann and I. Both were casually dressed for walking, wearing appropriate boots and carrying backpacks on their backs, just as Ann and I would have done. They looked happy as they walked arm in arm, away from the church and back down the hill towards the town. I felt anger and jealousy towards then. As we passed, they smiled at me and wished me a good morning. I did not acknowledge them and if they thought me rude, then so be it. How dare they smile when Ann is having surgery to remove her breast!

Entering the church, I saw that it was devoid of people. It was peaceful inside and I was grateful to be alone. Recorded music, with celestial singing was being played softly in the background, from somewhere in the church. My pace was much slower as I blindly walked around the church's inner sanctuary. Selecting a pew on the side aisle, facing the altar, I sat down on the wooden bench. I was tired, not from the walk but from the lack of sleep that had been denied the both of us over the last few nights as we had waited for this day to come. A combination of feelings including guilt, anger and worry, filled my head and with my hands covering my face, I began to cry. I lost all self-control, giving way to tears that filled my eyes and trickled down my face. I had forgotten to equip myself with a handkerchief that morning and used my hands and sleeves to wipe away the moisture that accumulated upon my face. I don't know how long I sat there, wallowing in my grief when suddenly I became aware that I was no longer alone, for someone had sat down beside me. I had not heard anyone approaching. Feeling embarrassed, that I should be seen in this way, I quickly tried to compose myself.

"Beautiful church isn't it," stated the voice of a man.

"Yes, I suppose it is."

Quite honestly, I had not taken much notice of the church's interior but as my eyes became clear, I looked around and saw that indeed it was beautiful, both architecturally, with its vaulted ceiling roof and gold bosses;

and naturally, with the colours of the wall hangings and picturesque stained glass windows.

"We are lucky that the church still stands and was not destroyed in the war from the enemy bombs. Did you know that a bomb landed quite close to our church? Some of the windows were smashed and tiles came off the roof but there was no structural damage done – just small repairs and a lot of clearing up to do."

Turning my attention to the gentleman sitting next to me, I was surprised to see that he was younger than I had expected. His conversation on the war might have led me to believe that he had known from experience, of the church's history. I concluded, however, that he was probably one of those church guides who welcomed visitors into their church and were able to give them a history lesson. He was smartly dressed but his clothing was old-fashioned. He wore a casual tweed jacket which had patches on the elbows. On closer inspection, I could see darn repairs to the front of his jacket and his shirt was slightly worn around the collar. On his head, he wore a flat cap and I wondered why he had not removed this on entering the church.

"Do you come here often?" I knew it was a silly thing to ask but I did not know what to say to him.

"I sometimes visit, I have always loved this church. When I was a young boy, I used to sing in the choir here. What about yourself?"

"No, I came in by chance. I'm waiting for my wife who's having surgery in the hospital here."

I didn't know why I had told him this information.

"The church is a good place when you are looking for solitude. It's much quieter than it used to be. Not so many visitors any more, but I guess that's to do with the change of time."

"Yes, I suppose you're right."

I took another glance at the man. He appeared quite muscular and fit and I wondered what his occupation might have been. He just sat there, looking forward, towards the altar. His head was tilted up slightly. He seemed to be studying the window above the altar, which depicted the resurrection of Christ.

"Beautiful window, isn't it?"

"Yes," I agreed, as I turned my attention to the stained glass window which filled the area both behind and above the altar. The sun must have been directly behind it as the figure of Christ was surrounded by a translucent golden colour. I don't think I have seen anything more beautiful and it was breath-taking to look at.

As the sun disappeared, probably behind a cloud, the church became a little darker and my senses were jogged back into the present. I looked at my watch to establish the time and turned towards the man.

"I guess I should be going now."

"You know, you must not blame yourself for the way you feel. I believe you are a good person and will look after Rosemary."

*How odd,* I thought, *for a complete stranger to say this to me.* Did he really just refer to my wife by her name or had I imagined it? I did not recall mentioning her by name in the short conversation we had had. Perhaps he had thought that he knew me or had been confusing me with someone else. Standing up to leave, I said goodbye quickly and walked back down the centre aisle, pausing only briefly to turn around and take a final look at the man; however, he was not there. The pew was empty. My eyes scoured the church to find him. Other than me, the church was empty. The music, now with a choir singing softly, was haunting.

# Chapter 3

The operation had been completed. The affected breast had been removed. Ann was left with a disfigurement that we would both find hard to deal with.

While Ann slept, the surgeon had asked to speak to me. He seemed so matter of fact about the surgery. He explained that he had removed, not only the breast but had taken lymph nodes from under her arm as well.

"I believe we have got all the cancer and Ann will recover well. A course of therapy will be advised to make sure that it is all gone. She will need you to be strong. When women have this sort of radical surgery, they can find it difficult to cope with mentally. As I mentioned to you before, the team are here to support you, so don't hesitate to call on their expertise."

When Ann awoke, that afternoon, she seemed in good spirits but as the pain relief wore off, she became more tearful and withdrawn. The nurse advised me to be there for the first change of dressings to the wound that had been left. Ann was at first unsure if she wanted me to be there but I reassured her that I should stay. We had discussed this well before the operation and had decided that we would face everything together. It was, in all honesty, the worst day of my life but I had to appear optimistic in Ann's presence. This was not going to be an easy thing to do!

I thought about the man I had seen in church the day before. He had called me a good person.

With sweaty hands, I stood watching the nurse as she removed the dressings. The bloody stained material was discarded into a bag at the side of her trolley. Ann had asked for a mirror so that she could see what I could see. The nurse had wanted her to be prepared for the thick swollen red folds of skin that had been neatly sutured together.

"It will take time for the swelling to go down. Mr Monro is one of our best surgeons. His stitching is always small and neat. Just have patience, my dear, for it will improve."

My brave Ann coped admirably and I felt so proud of her. With time, the physical wounds would heal. A course of treatment followed. During this time, she had not only lost her breast but then her hair started to fall out. There is only so much joking about one's self appearance that can be made.

Dark days, filled with periods of silence or tears, eventually turned into brighter ones as my Ann recovered. Daily, I also became stronger and more optimistic. I had come to realise that this illness was all about Ann and not me. She was the one who had suffered the pain and discomfort. She was the one who would live with the disfigurement and yet, she remained the stronger of the two of us. I was proud of the way she had coped with everything.

Life got better and eventually, we returned to a near-normal life. She was mentally whole again. The physical side to our relationship took longer to repair. I was determined to let Ann take her time and waited eagerly for her to make that first move. But after what seemed like ages to me, but had in all honesty been but a few short weeks, I decided that perhaps it was me that should broach the subject of having sex again. Ann held back with a shyness I had not seen since the first time we met. It was like a courtship all over again, which excited me. Beginning with kissing and fondling, in time we became more adventurous and explored, more sensually, the most intimate parts of the body that exhibited gratification from each other's touch. The prosthesis that Ann held firmly to her chest eventually gave way to her needs and mine.

It seemed that all would be well but our happiness was to be short-lived when the cancer cells returned and this time could not be beaten. *How cruel,* I had thought, *when Ann had worked so hard trying to fight off her cancer.* We had become more optimistic and life was good again. I know she found it difficult to tell me the results of her tests. We did not go to bed that night but sat up, cuddled together on the couch. Ann wept in my arms and I struggled again to find the right words to comfort her. When she could cry no more, she became angry.

"Dear God! Why me! What have I done to deserve this?"

In the days that followed, Ann began to show gradual signs of acceptance and turned her focus onto planning for the inevitable end. In those first few weeks, following that devastating news, Ann had felt fairly well, although she was very tired. We spent hours talking together, making plans just as she had wanted. I wondered how many people, that knew that they were dying, felt the need to do this. It all seemed so morbid.

She remained stalwart.

"I must get everything organised before it takes over my life and I can no longer cope."

When the pain started, things were about to change.

Sometimes, I would lay awake at night listening to her crying. She sobbed quietly, so as not to draw attention to herself. I knew she wanted me to believe in her acceptance of a premature death and I respected her for this and went along with it.

Daily, I watched her as she began to go downhill. The cancer was slowly taking my Ann away from me and I was losing my fun-loving, beautiful partner.

The last few weeks, before her death, she had not been able to leave the house – I could only watch on as her pain increased and her energy levels subsided and she started to lose weight. Afraid to leave her on her own, the family came together. First Lottie and then Mathew. Between us, and with Ann's friend Jill, we managed to take care of her at home. This had been her one hope.

Ann took to her bed completely, for two weeks, before she was to leave us bereft. During that time, she was given increasing amounts of morphine to control her pain. She would have strange, vivid dreams and hallucinations. Other times she would be agitated, confused or sleepy. The night she died, I had been upstairs. I heard voices coming from downstairs. Ann was in conversation with someone. Going to her side, she appeared to be sleeping and very relaxed. I saw happiness in her facial expression, gone were the telltale signs of pain. Instinctively, I knew her time was near. Kneeling by her side, I took her hands in mine. I wanted her to know that she was not alone.

"My darling Ann, I am here with you. I love you always."

Tears welled in my eyes and rolled down my face. Ann tried to lift her hand to me but all her strength had gone. Ann was at peace. No more suffering. No more pain. The cancer had done its worst and had taken my greatest love away from me.

# Chapter 4

I had been told to expect some side effects from the drugs that Ann had been given. However, I was to question some of the things that she had told me, some of the things that she had witnessed. I knew she was a strong person and that under normal circumstances, would not have accepted the things that she believed she had seen, at least not without further investigation.

I began to question some of the details that she had confided to me and I know that sometimes, I had made her angry with my rational responses.

The day that Ruth came into our lives was just as much a surprise to me as it was to Ann. For Ruth had indeed born some resemblance to Ann. We only met on that one occasion, when she visited Ann. At first, I just thought it a coincidence and didn't think any more about it after she had left. It was a busy time in the house; what with John and Jean's visit and the news of Lottie's pregnancy. I suppose I put it to the back of my mind.

It was the day of Ann's funeral that I was to meet Ruth again. At the end of the service, just like everyone else, she came and offered her condolences and said that she had felt close to Ann but could not explain why especially given the fact that she had only met her on that one occasion. She told me that Rosemary Thorne, from the priory, had died on the same day as Ann and she wondered if I had known her. The sisters had told Ruth that Ann's mother, Ruby, had been very fond of Miss Thorn and had visited her often. I remembered that my mother-in-law had indeed spent a lot of her time, in her later years, helping in the priory. I was rather taken aback with Ruth's next statement though.

"When I saw Miss Thorn, the day before she died, she called me Rosemary again. She also cried out for Ruby."

This all seemed very strange.

"What a coincidence. And you say she was a nurse who had lived in this village during the war?"

"Yes, she was my nurse tutor in London. She told me that she also knew my parents, who had come from this same village."

Now was not the time to discuss this further so I suggested that we could meet up the following week, for a chat and made arrangements to meet in the coffee shop.

There were too many things that did not add up and too many things that needed to be explained.

The church of St Edmund's was full of people that came to say goodbye to Ann. Friends from the village and the church, as well as those from the hospital that she had worked in. My brother-in-law John and his wife Jean were also able to attend. The day had been a difficult one, especially for our children. We all knew that this day had been looming over our heads, but none of us was prepared for the impact the day would have on us. We had been particularly upset that Ann did not see Christmas, as was her last wish. The service was followed by a private cremation for close family and friends.

The Reverend Richard Denby had taken Ann through the completed journey.

Two days later, and on my own, I took her ashes to the churchyard and scattered them across the grave where her grandparents had been buried. This was where the ashes of her mother, and brother, Douglas, were also scattered and had been her wish as well. She would be at peace now, with the family she had loved and grown up with. No more suffering. No more pain.

Ruth had agreed to meet with me in the village coffee shop at ten o'clock. Having arrived a little early, I sat in a window seat with a coffee and watched as the village came to life. Even for a small village, there could be a lot of traffic passing through, the plans for a bypass having yet to be passed. From the window and in the distance, it was possible to see the primary children taking exercise in the field behind the school. Heavy snow had fallen, two days previous and the remnants of melted slush were still visible in places. The wind was cold and blowing from an easterly direction. Further snow had been forecast in the next twenty-four hours. Shoppers were busy purchasing supplies, just in case, they could not get out for a while. I watched as a young woman was pushing a crying baby in a pram. At her side was a little boy being hurried along, complaining that he was unable to walk anymore.

I thought of Lottie and how she would cope with being a mother. She is so like Ann that I believe she will take to parenting very easily. Without her mother, she might need my help and I am determined to be a good grandfather.

On the other side of the road, I could see Ann approaching but quickly corrected myself as it was Ruth that I was seeing and I watched as she safely crossed the road. *How uncanny,* I thought.

The similarities between Ann and Ruth were quite incredible, even just by the way she was walking, sprightly and upright with an air of confidence about her. Her hair was tucked under a woollen hat just as Ann would have done on a cold day like today. I stood up as she approached. She took hold of my hands and pulled me closer to plant a kiss on my cheek.

"It's cold out there today. More snow to come, so I've heard."

"Yes," I had agreed, rather bemused that she had greeted me with a kiss. "How do you take your coffee, Ruth?"

"Black with no sugar please," came the reply.

I shouldn't have expected her to say anything different as this was the way Ann had always taken her coffee.

Buying two coffees, as I had completed my first one, I returned to the table that I had been sitting at. Ruth had taken my seat so I sat in the one opposite her.

"I hope you don't mind if I sit here. I don't like having my back to the door. Silly really, I know, but it's just something I always do."

"I don't mind at all," I replied, wondering how she would feel if I told her that Ann had always done the same thing.

"How are you, Jamie?"

"I'm OK, thanks. I still have lots to sort out, which is a good thing, as it keeps me busy."

I watch as Ruth sips the hot black coffee and then quickly realise that I am staring at her as our eyes meet. Putting down her cup, she sits back in the chair.

"So, Jamie, what is it you want to know?"

I had forgotten that it was I who had asked to meet. She must have thought me a little strange. Without giving too much away, I asked her if she would repeat what she had told me at the funeral regarding this Miss Thorne. She was eager to share with me the details regarding her relationship with the lady in question and I wondered if she herself suspected that things were not quite as they seemed and that something had been amiss.

I learnt that Ruth had first met Rosemary Thorne in London when she was training to be a nurse. Miss Thorne had been her tutor and had taken her under her wing. Ruth had been going through a difficult time when an old boyfriend had left her and gone off with her best friend. Ruth considered giving up on her nurse training and Sister Thorne, as she was known, managed to persuade her to stay and complete the course. They had become friends. It was only when she had taken Miss Thorne to meet her Auntie Irene, and the two ladies had recognised each other, that Ruth found out that Miss Thorne had known her parents as well from back when she lived here in this village, both before and during the war. However, she did seem surprised that the vicar and his wife at that time had had a child.

"We lost contact when I qualified and I later heard that she had retired to Sussex. I had no idea that she had come back to this village, where she had originally come from. It was quite a shock meeting her again when I was asked to visit her in the priory."

"You mentioned that she called you Rosemary."

"Yes, but Sister Margaret had explained to me that she had bouts of memory loss and confusion."

I wondered if she knew that Ann's name had been Rosemary before she changed it but decided that I should, for the time being, keep this to myself. I thought again about the rather strange dream that Ann had had regarding her birth, the one she eventually told to me. I was then wondering if Ruth and Ann could possibly be related in some way?

"Do you know when Rosemary Thorne's funeral is to be held? Or has it already taken place?" I asked.

"It's tomorrow afternoon. There are unlikely to be many people there except for the nuns from the priory. I don't think she knew many people. Naturally, I will go," she paused for a while and appeared to study me before she continued, "can I ask you why you are so interested?"

Thinking carefully about my reply, as I do not want to say too much before I can be certain of the facts, I explained, "In the last few weeks, before Ann died, she had strange dreams and hallucinations. We both knew that they were probably caused by the large doses of morphine she was given. I know it sounds ridiculous but some of the things that she told me are beginning to make sense."

"Well, if I can help in any way, don't be afraid to ask. I only have one more week before I return to London. I'm going to miss this place but I am looking forward to spending more than a weekend with my husband again."

Ruth drained the last of her, now luke-warm, coffee from the cup. From her handbag, she took out a pair of colourful knitted gloves and put them on. She sees that I am watching her.

"They were a Christmas present from a grateful patient."

We walked out into the chilly air together. I realise that I feel so at ease with Ruth and I reciprocate her early cheek kiss with another.

"Take care, Ruth. It's been lovely meeting you."

"You too, Jamie. I hope you find the answers you are looking for."

With that, we walked away in opposite directions. It was very unlikely that we would ever meet again.

# Chapter 5

The walk back along the potholed lane, which led out of the village, might have been to some people, treacherous. The snow had not been cleared from the smaller infrequently used roads. A combination of slushy snow and mud meant that it was slippery underfoot. It was fortunate that I knew the lane well, including every bit of uneven surface that I walked. Pacing myself, slower than I normally would walk, it gave me time to think about the recent events.

In her final hours, Ann had told me that she was happy now because she had understood everything. I never knew what she had been referring to and thought that the morphine was causing her to be confused.

I had decided that I had nothing to lose so would phone the Priory that afternoon and make an appointment to see Sister Margaret.

I was not sure if I was doing the right thing. What might I find out? What effect would it have on those I love if there had been foul play? The expression, 'let sleeping dogs lie' kept playing on my mind. Curiosity and the need for some closure, however, got the better of me and with slightly shaky hands, I dialled the number for the priory. A woman's voice answered.

"Hello, Sister Margaret speaking, how can I help you?"

From the sound of her voice, I imagined this lady to be a kind and genteel person. Someone I could happily talk to.

"You probably don't know me, my name is James Johnson. I live in the village. I wondered if I could come and see you. My mother in law was Ruby –"

Before I could say her surname, Sister Margaret had interrupted me. "Yes, of course, I would love to meet you. Sadly, it will have to wait till next week as regrettably, I have a full diary."

We both concurred a suitable day to meet the following week.

I would have to remain patient until then.

I did not realise that there was so much to do when someone dies. Ann had been quite methodical in her preparation for this time. She had written down everything that had been important to her and had left her notes in my care. There were financial things to settle as she had accounts in her own name. There had also been personal bequests to family and friends. She had personalised letters for both Lottie and Mathew and they had been comforted by them. In them, she made reference to her forth-coming grandchild, stating how she knew that the baby will be much loved and what wonderful parents Lottie and Pete would make. For me, there had been nothing and I had not expected anything. We had spoken often and everything was said that needed to be said; memories, and my family around me, were all I would ever need. I knew that Ann would always be with me in spirit and I was comforted with that thought. I suppose you could say, I was prepared for Ann's death and had been secretly mourning her as I watched her gradually slip away from me.

Jill had been the very best of friends. She continued helping me through the days after the funeral. Her relationship with Ann was one of love and trust and for this, I was grateful. At the funeral, she was composed, just as Ann had requested, but afterwards had been difficult to console. I began to notice that she was looking very tired and had to remind her that she had fulfilled her commitments to Ann tenfold and that it was time for her to take a step back.

"I promised Ann that I would take care of you all," she had insisted.

"It's time to let go, Jill. You have been a good friend to both of us but I think you will make yourself ill if you go on as you are. I know that Ann would not have wanted that."

"Will you promise to call me if you need anything at all?"

"Of course I will. Now go and spend some time with your family. I will be fine."

Ann had asked me to give Jill the crystal necklace that she had worn often and Jill had always admired. This I did which only made her cry again.

Christmas and New Year had come and gone. This was Ann's favourite time of the year. No matter how hard we tried to celebrate, as she had wished, we could not do her justice. As a family, we spent some time together, quietly in reflection. Pete once again insisted that we had Christmas lunch together in his restaurant. The restaurant was closed for the season so it would be just the family. I insisted that both Lottie and Mathew spent time with their partners and their respective families. They were both difficult to persuade.

"You must do this for both your mother and I. I need some time on my own."

Lottie tried to argue her case to stay with me.

"I don't want you to be on your own. It's too soon."

There was no way I could be persuaded. The time spent alone gave me the privacy to grieve. That was what I desperately needed.

I decided it was time to sort through the growing pile of paperwork that had accumulated over the recent weeks. It was also time to catch up on some work that had fallen behind schedule. The room had become untidy as I had neglected it. An assortment of papers had been put to one side to dry where I had managed to spill my coffee over them. On the chair was an assortment of sympathy cards, which I had hastily taken down as I could no longer bear to look at them. I promised myself that I would read them again before destroying them, but I had no taste for it yet. In the corner of the room was the wheelchair, which Jill had obviously forgotten to take away, and I did not want to trouble her. On the chair was the patchwork cushion that Lottie had made. Underneath the cushion I saw, sticking out, the photograph album that John had given to Ann.

Retrieving the book, I pushed aside some papers on the desk and carefully turned the pages, aware that some of its contents were fragile. Pictures of Ann and her family stared back at me. Lottie was so like her mother in appearance, as a small child. I wondered what my grandchild might look like when it is of a similar age. Turning the next page, I came upon a picture that appeared to be a party or celebration for something. The black and white photograph had been folded in half at some point. The crease down the middle meant that some of the faces had become distorted. The picture depicted rows of trestle tables in, possibly, a village hall. Adults and children alike were enjoying themselves. On closer inspection, I could see that bunting had been strung across the room. Some of the individuals appeared to be holding small union flags. In conclusion, I believed that the party was none other than a celebration held when the war was over. At the head of the middle table stood a tall man wearing a white collar and I presumed that he was a priest or vicar. In his hand, he held a glass and it appeared that he was in the process of making a speech. In the forefront of a side table, I could make out, who I thought could be, Douglas and John, sitting together. Standing behind them were a man and woman who I thought could possibly be Ruby and Daniel. In the arms of the man was a small child. Could this be my Ann, I had wondered? I don't know why I did, but I scoured the picture for other small children. Most of the children had been of similar ages or sizes to Douglas and John. However, standing at the back was a lady holding a small child of similar proportions to the young Ann. I wished I had seen this before and had asked John if he had recognised anyone in that particular photograph.

John and Jean had delayed their journey home to Australia until after the funeral but had to leave the following day. I had already decided to give the album to Mathew. I knew that he would enjoy the old photographs far more than I would and could keep them for the next generation. Carefully, I removed the photograph that I had been studying and placed it in an envelope.

The sound of the telephone ringing startled me and I dropped the envelope to the floor.

"Good afternoon, my name is Sister Margaret. I am phoning from the priory. Can I speak to Mr Johnson please?"

"Yes, James Johnson speaking." I was not due to visit the priory until the end of the week.

"Mr Johnson, I know you have asked to see me and that we have an appointment this coming Friday, but something has come up and I wondered if you would be able to visit me this afternoon instead?"

I looked at my watch and it was already after three o'clock. Before I could respond, Sister Margaret continued and sounded rather anxious.

"It is really important for me to see you. Shall we say four-thirty?"

"Yes, I can be there."

"Thank you, I will look forward to seeing you then."

With just over an hour to get to my meeting with Sister Margaret, I decided that if I left soon then I would have time to walk to the priory. I safely placed the envelope, containing the fragile photograph, in the inside pocket of my coat.

Taking a torch with me, as I knew that it would start to get dark early, I left the house. The fresh air and exercise would be beneficial as I had been sitting at my desk for several hours. It was bitterly cold outside and I pulled up my collar to keep out the winter chill, increasing my pace as I did so. Briskly walking along, I wondered whether Sister Margaret would remember me. It had been a few years but I had previously done some work for the priory. Some renovations were needed to secure a large, outbuilding in the gardens and Ann's mother asked if I could help. My services were conducted free of any payment, as the priory at this time had been short of funds. As I had been in between jobs, I was happy to help out.

Arriving punctually, I rang the bell and eagerly waited for someone to respond.

It was Sister Margaret herself that was to greet me at the door and I was shown into her office. She was a lot older than I remembered and appeared to walk with a limp. She had greeted me with a warm smile but I could see that she was experiencing some pain. I considered myself to be quite an expert now at reading people's faces when they were in pain.

"Thank you for coming, Mr Johnson. I believe we have met before."

She seemed genuinely pleased to see me. I told her about the work I had done a few years ago for the priory.

"Yes of course. It was your mother-in-law, Ruby, who introduced us. You were very generous and as I remember, would not take any payment for your work."

"It was so many years ago now, Sister and I was glad I could help."

Seated opposite Sister Margaret, as she sat at her desk, I was again reminded of another face in pain. She seemed to know what I was thinking.

"I'm getting old now and with age come mild ailments."

From her pocket, she took a small bunch of keys and began to unlock the desk drawer. From the drawer, she removed a white envelope from the top of a pile of neat papers.

"Mr Johnson," she started.

"Please, call me Jamie," I invited and she smiled at me.

"Jamie, I know you have recently lost your wife Rosemary and in sad circumstances. I believe she had been very unwell and I am truly sorry for your loss."

"Thank you, Sister."

"You must be wondering why I have asked to see you so urgently. I will get to the point straight away but I am

192

wondering if what I tell you will not be of a surprise to you at all especially as you had requested to meet with me."

By this stage, I was finding it hard to contain what I was indeed thinking and I was curious to hear what she had to tell me.

"Jamie, I knew your mother-in-law, Ruby, very well. She was a lovely woman and she spent a lot of her time helping us here in the priory. She became great friends with a lady here named Rosemary Thorne. I don't know whether you knew of her."

For now, I decided to keep what little I did know to myself. It wasn't as if I was being untruthful, because anything I did know was just a suspicion. I could answer honestly.

"No, I didn't know this lady."

Sister Margaret seemed content with my reply and continued.

"Sadly, Rosemary Thorne died recently. Coincidently, I believe it was the same day that your wife passed away."

For a moment, I wondered how she would have known that until I remembered that Ruth had been looking after this lady as well as visiting Ann.

"That is a coincidence," I agreed.

"For a few years, before she died, Rosemary had suffered from a form of dementia. This had got increasingly worse after she lost her best friend, Ruby. In fact, she became very withdrawn. In her youth, she had worked her whole life as a nurse and was aware that her memory was fading. Shortly after Ruby's death, she wrote a letter which she gave to me for safekeeping. I was instructed to only open it on her death.

In all honesty, I had forgotten about it until I was going through her papers."

This was indeed intriguing and I was aware that my pulse was quickening. I didn't want to appear rude but I was wishing to myself that she would get to the point. Pausing for a moment, she looked at me as if she could read what I was thinking.

"What was in the letter?" I could no longer contain myself and had spoken out before she could continue.

"The letter to me was more of a confession. I believe that after she had written it, she had tried to talk to me on this subject but in her confused state and memory loss, she had found difficulty in finding the right words. The few words she managed to speak were of guilt and regret. In my heart, I always knew something was amiss and prayed that one day she would speak to me. Everyone living with us in the priory, without exception, have their own right to privacy. As a nun, I can listen to spiritual confessions and I am sure that you would understand that if anything was disclosed to me, I would be bound by my faith."

Now, I thought to myself that she will not be able to disclose the contents of the letter.

"So why," I asked myself, "is she telling me all this?"

"I quite understand what you are saying but where do I fit into this?"

"The letter that had been written to me, I will, for now, keep as a confession. However, there was a second letter among her effects. It is addressed to, I believe, your wife, Mrs Rosemary Johnson. At first, I did not realise that it was your wife as Ruby always referred to her daughter as Ann. It was only when I spoke with the nurses from the palliative care team, who helped to care for Rosemary, that I became aware of your wife's birth name."

My hands became sweaty as my heart beat faster and I felt the need to dry them on my trousers. My mouth was dry and I found it difficult to swallow.

"Jamie, let me get you some water."

Sister Margaret was obviously aware of my predicament, brought on by what she was telling me.

I was filled with a mixture of excitement and anticipation. I watched her as she crossed the room to the dark wooden antique sideboard, standing in front of the lattice window, a tray, containing two glasses and a carafe of water, stood next to a selection of religious ornaments. She used both hands to pour the water into a glass. Walking back towards me, I was again reminded of her limp and the pain that she was probably suffering and I felt guilty that I had needed the water.

"Thank you," I said in a soft tone of voice, as I took the glass from her in my shaky hand. The first sip stuck in my throat, a second one moistened my mouth as it went down and I felt easier.

"Shall I continue now?"

"Yes, please do."

"Now, I know the contents of my letter, I can only assume that the letter to your wife holds similar information. With your wife sadly passed on, I was not sure what I should do with this letter. I have prayed hard for guidance and have come to the conclusion that I should give it to you. I hope that when you have read its contents, you will know what, if anything, needs to be done."

Again, she opened her desk drawer, took out a second envelope and handed it to me.

"I will leave you in peace now to read your letter. The door behind you, to the right, leads out to the garden of tranquillity and you are welcome to walk its paths should you so wish. There are lights along its pathway."

I knew it would be cold outside and the early evening was drawing ever nearer but I was interested to see the garden. With my winter coat still on, as I had not removed it when I came in, due to the chilly temperature of the room, I replaced my scarf and gloves and headed out of the door, the letter held firmly in my gloved hand.

The garden was completely quiet. Small lights did indeed light the way down its cobbled path. On the first impression, the garden of tranquillity appeared to me to be bare, with very little colour, save for a selection of evergreen bushes that intermingled with the larger deciduous trees, but on closer inspection, I saw that it was getting ready to burst into new life. Bulbs were shooting up uniformly on either side of the pathway. Behind the bulbs lay an assortment of shrubs, showing the beginnings of new growth with their small buds. As I walked a little further down the path, I came across a large patch of ground that was covered with snowdrops in full bloom. These were one of Ann's favourite spring flowers and they looked stunning. After a few more steps, I came across a stone inglenook and decided that this was the place to sit and read my letter and it was in full sight of the flowers. I found it necessary to remove my gloves to open the letter, which had been folded in half before being placed in its protective envelope. Taking out my spectacles, from an inside pocket of my coat, I started to read…

## THE LETTER

*My dearest Rosemary,*

*If you are reading this letter, it is because I am no longer here. God will, therefore, be my judge.*

*Before I tell you what has caused me so much heartache, all my life, I need you to know that I confessed what I knew to your mother; my dearest friend Ruby, and that she gave me forgiveness. She was one of the kindest people I have ever had the privilege to know. Just like your grandmother, Megan, who I also loved dearly. It was Megan, who treated me like one of her own family, whom I owe most to.*

*By the time I discovered what I am about to tell you, your grandmother had sadly passed away. I hope that we will meet up again in heaven.*

*The night you were born, I had been unable to be with your family, this was due to an air raid. We were lucky compared with many other towns and villages and did not suffer the Luftwaffe bombs often. I tried to get to your mother but became caught up with casualties from an explosion when an enemy aircraft crashed into a house in the village. Several people were in the house at the time, including three children who were evacuees from London. They had taken refuge under the dining table while others in the house hid under the stairs. Sadly, two of the young children lost their lives, as well as two older members of the family that had taken them in. It was a horrific sight. I was torn between my duty, to attend your mother in labour and the devastation that the air crash had caused but knew you would be in safe hands with your grandmother. She had been present for the birth of both your brothers and I had often told her that she would make a good and caring nurse.*

*It would be with great regret and guilt that I was not there at the time of your birth because, my dearest Rosemary, we did not know that your mother was carrying twins. She was not due to deliver for another four weeks. Nature had obviously intervened and when I examined your mother, she was indeed in the early stages of labour.*

*My dearest Rosemary, what I am about to tell you now is the testament from your grandmother. You were the first to be born; a healthy but small baby, in comparison with your brothers. Your twin sister was much smaller and weaker and no matter how hard your grandmother tried to save her, she did not make it. When I finally got to your mother, she had lost a lot of blood and on seeing that you were well, my priority was to get Ruby to the hospital for a blood transfusion. Your mother was very unwell and I was concerned about her.*

Pausing a while, I tried to imagine the scene that was now set out before me. So, my Ann was one of a twin and somehow she had known this. At least, I now knew that my suspicions, regarding Ruth, were justified. I read on but felt intrusive at doing so.

*It was the following day that I visited Megan in her home. I needed to check the details of the delivery again. I also had a duty of care to see that she was alright after her ordeal. She was to tell me that, at first, she did not know what to do about the dead baby – but decided to call on the help of Rev. Coombes. He was a kind and respected man of the community*

198

*and had been a close friend of the family. Megan had wanted to protect her family. No one needed to know what had happened. There was already much sadness in the chaos that the war had brought to the village. Both Megan and Ruby decided that it was not necessary to tell anyone else in the family, but I do know that Megan did confide in your grandfather and I am glad she did.*

*For my part, I kept quiet on the matter. The authorities would never need to know. As far as we were aware, The Rev. Coombes buried the baby in a quiet spot in the churchyard and as far as I know, no one else knew where this was.*

*Many people believe that twins have a special bond between them and I often wondered if you would grow up with any of these feelings. I was delighted when your parents chose to name you after me and I watched you grow into a sturdy young infant, much of this because of your older brothers that took you under their wing and protected you.*

*The war took away my only true love. Like countless others, he was killed in battle and I was devastated. After the war, I turned to my career for solace and went to London to continue with my nursing. Caught up with changes that nursing had to adapt to, I threw myself into my work. In later years, I became a nurse tutor. Contact between your family and myself dwindled. I think most of it was down to me. Regular letters from your grandmother turned into annual Christmas cards and when I heard that she had passed away, I knew that it was time to let go.*

*Things were about to change again when I met a young girl who was training to be a nurse. She was struggling a bit and did not seem particularly happy. I had observed her with patients and knew that she had something special to offer in* nursing. One day, she told me that she was considering giving up her training. There was something familiar about her and I was keen to help. We talked a lot and became friends. Being someone old enough to be her mother, I found myself taking on this role.

One day, after work, I had given her a lift home and she invited me in to meet her Auntie Irene. She had told me that her Aunt had been like a second mother to her, her parents having been killed in a motor accident when she was in her teens. Irene welcomed me into her home and thanked me for keeping an eye on Ruth. She had also realised that Ruth was going to be a great nurse one day. As we talked over a cup of tea, we came to realise that we had met before. At first, I was delighted. Here was someone that I knew from Sussex during the war.

She was none other than the sister of Rev. Coombes, who came from London with her baby to be away from the blitz. I remembered her well as she had often helped her brother in the church. I wondered what had become of her baby.

Ruth left the room to refresh the pot of tea so I thought I would enquire after her own child. Treading carefully, in case all was not well, I asked her where her own daughter lived. Nothing could have prepared me for the shock I was to have. She told me that Ruth was that baby.

'She was never really mine,' she had said, 'she was the child of my brother and his wife. They asked me to come and help look after her when she was born. They were busy people; what with looking after the evacuees sent out from London and parish duties, and of course I was happy to be out of the city.'

*Had I indeed misunderstood her? Surely my memory couldn't have been that bad, for I could have sworn that the vicar's wife could not have been the mother of Ruth – as she had once told me that she was unable to have children of her own. I can still recall the specific time that she had told me this. I was helping her in the village hall as she, with the other ladies from the church, prepared for the arrival of more evacuees. The vicar and his wife had agreed to take in three young children from the same family that had been evacuated from London. She had said that the vicarage was a large house and needed to be filled with children.*

*Ruth reappeared, carrying another steaming pot of tea, but I made my excuses to getaway. I needed to think things through.*

*The following day, however, I decided to visit Ruth's Auntie Irene again. I did this without Ruth knowing. I was again welcomed into the house. This time, however, I was after more clarity regarding Ruth's upbringing and was not to be disappointed.*

*Irene told me how much she had loved Ruth. Even as a baby, she had spent more time with her than her own mother had. She happily retold to me how Ruth had started to call her 'mama'. 'Don't get me wrong,' she had said, her parents doted on her as well. She went on to tell me that she had never married but that she would have loved to have had children of her own.*

*It was then that she proceeded to tell me that Ruth had been born during an air raid and that she nearly didn't make it. She told me that her sister-in-law had gone into early labour and that Ruth was a very tiny baby that had needed a lot of care. Her brother and sister-in-law were so happy but* concerned that baby Ruth would not live. She had wished that she could have been with them when Ruth was born.

So now I knew the truth. What I should do with that truth, I did not know. As time went by, I decided to do nothing. Both Irene and Ruth were happy. Contact with your family had all but ceased. The Rev. Coombes, who had taken your twin sister away from your grandmother, had obviously noticed that she still had life in her. In a way, I suppose you could say he saved her life. Why he had chosen to keep the baby, I guess we will never know. I do remember that his wife seemed to be a little more distant towards me when we had met on a second occasion in the church hall. It was on that day that she had told me about her husband's sister who was coming from London to stay in the vicarage, to help look after the children in her care.

It was years later that I made the decision to retire back to Sussex. My health was declining. Age was catching me up and I had no family, to my knowledge, and did not want to be alone. I approached Sister Margaret, in the priory. She had remembered me and took me in willingly and I worked alongside the three nuns that lived in the priory at that time. I helped to nurse the two elderly residents that resided there at that time. When I became too old for physical work, I spent my time doing other chores, helping in the kitchen and the gardens, where ever I could from my wheelchair. The small amount that I had saved had been given to the priory in return for my accommodation and care in old age. In later years, I spent most of my time in the seclusion of my room. It was during this time that I was to meet your mother Ruby again.

Our friendship was rekindled and I was to learn all that had happened to you. She showed me photographs of your *family and kept me updated with your news. My own health was deteriorating fast and I knew that I needed to tell your mother the secret I had kept from her. She remained quiet as I divulged all that I knew. I was amazed by her reaction. I didn't know what I was expecting. She thanked me for telling her. Being so practical minded, she decided that it was not necessary to tell anyone else. I enjoyed your mother's company and friendship until the day she was suddenly taken away from us.*

*Once again, I had lost my dearest friend and felt I had nothing more to live for. I knew that I was becoming increasingly forgetful and that is why I decided to write this letter and give it to Sister Margaret for safekeeping. So, my dear Rosemary, now you know the whole story. What you decide to do with it is up to you.*

*Ruth was an amazing nurse. I know she married and became a mother herself. I no longer have contact with her but I believe she still lives in London. Forgive me for not wanting to see you in person. I have always thought of you with the fondest love and know that you are happy. I only hope that when you read this letter you will not think too cruelly of me and in time can find it in your heart to forgive me.*

The letter was signed off with affectionate words.

How glad I was to have chosen to read the letter on my own and in the privacy of the garden. I was no longer able to hold back the tears as I felt overwhelmingly saddened by the letter. My tears were for Rosemary Thorne, who I never knew until now, and for Megan, who I never had the chance to meet. As the tears fell, I remembered Ruby who had been like a mother to me, but most of all, I cried for her daughter, Ann, who I have loved and now miss with all of my heart.

How long I sat there, wiping away my tears only for my eyes to fill and spill over and over again, I do not know. When I finally managed some composure, I realised that the sky was getting very dark. A figure walked towards me and I saw that it was Sister Margaret. She sat down beside me and took my cold hands into her own.

"You have obviously had a shock, Jamie. Will you be alright going home?"

"Yes, Sister, thank you for your kindness and for allowing me to read this letter. Can I tell you something?"

She smiled, teasingly at me. "Is it to be a confession?"

I could see from her face that she was trying to lighten my mood and I wondered how she would feel once I told her what I was about to say.

"I believe that before Ann died, she knew that Ruth was her twin sister. Both before, and during, her illness she had had many strange dreams and experienced apparitions and had described some of the events that are documented in detail in this letter. How could she possibly have known these things?"

Sister Margaret looked kindly and directly into my eyes before she spoke.

"If you are looking for answers, I am afraid I have none. Strange things happen all the time. I'm not sure we should question how or why they do. I believe that some things happen for a reason and are for the individual alone and the onlookers, like you, and I must accept these things without question. I will pray for you both."

"Thank you again, Sister, for your kindness."

"If you ever need to speak with me again, remember our door will always be open to you."

# Chapter 6

Stepping outside, into the cool evening air, I started to shiver. I pulled up my collar before I put on my hat and gloves. I was glad that I had remembered to bring a torch with me. The street lights would help me for the first part of my journey home but I knew that when I reached the lane I would most definitely need the torch. The village shops had closed up for the evening. Lights had been turned off. Two street lights, either end of the main street, had already come on, casting shadows across the paths. As I reached the end of the main street, I turned on my torch. The light was not very bright and it flickered now and again.

The battery power was obviously low and I reprimanded myself for not checking the torch before I left the house. My only other source of light was from the occasional passing car, which were quite sporadic at this time of the evening. I found the turning, taking me off the road and into the lane, fairly easily, but knew I would have to walk a little slower to avoid the potholes and slippery slush that was still evident. A second path from the lane led to the back of the village church. Ann had often used this path when she visited the churchyard, instead of walking into the village and entering the church grounds from the front. As I passed this small path, I carelessly stumbled and twisted my ankle, dropping my torch at the same time, swearing loudly, as the pain was excruciating. There was nothing to grab hold of, so I went down with my hands in front of me to steady myself. Standing again, I tried to put the injured foot to the ground. It was painful but I knew that the only way I would get home was to tolerate the pain and hobble the best I could. Bending down again, I tried to locate the torch but was unable to find it, "bloody hell," I swore again.

"Can I help you?"

A man's voice had spoken out of the darkness and had startled me. Looking up, I could see the tall outline shape of a figure standing at my side. I had not heard anyone approaching. I could not see his face clearly as he appeared to have a scarf that wrapped around him to keep out the cold. I definitely did not recognise his voice so assumed that he was a stranger to me.

"Thank you," I said, "I seem to have twisted my ankle and have dropped my torch at the same time."

As I stood uncomfortably next to him, I saw that he wore a sensible long black coat and a very large hat.

"Take hold of my arm and let me help you home."

He too seemed to be without a torch.

"I'm going your way and I know this path well."

As there are only two houses at the end of the lane, and one of those was my own, I could only surmise that the stranger was visiting my neighbour. Very few people walk this lane so I was surprised that this visitor had chosen to do so on a winter's evening like this. I was, however, glad that he had been there.

"Have you walked far?" I enquired as we walked together in close proximity.

"Not really," came the response, "I often walk this lane, through the back of the church."

I assumed, from his comment, that he was obviously a local man. I wondered why I had never met him before. The path before us was about to split into two. In front of me, I could see the outline of my house. The path to my right went to the only other house reached from this lane. Thinking that the stranger was visiting the other, I let go of his arm.

"Thank you again for your help. I think I will be able to manage now."

The gate was in reach and I lifted the latch to open it.

"You're very welcome, Jamie."

Stunned. Did he really say my name? I did not recall ever mentioning it to him. I turned to look again, at the man who had been so kind, but he was no longer there. I had thought that he must have been in a great hurry to visit my neighbour. How strange to meet someone who knew my name but that I had no recognition of. I was tired and my foot was throbbing. I was desperate to get inside the sanctuary of my house.

Taking the bunch of keys out of my coat pocket, I quickly identified the appropriate door key and let myself into the house and turned on the light. Dropping my coat and hat on the chair in the hallway, I hobbled into the kitchen. Reaching for the bottle of whisky, I poured a very large glass full and downed it in one. From the freezer, I took out a bag of frozen peas, just as Ann would have done. With the bottle of whisky and the empty glass in one hand and the bag of peas in the other, I hobbled back into the lounge. A few more painful steps before I slumped down into my favourite worn leather armchair. It was painful removing the shoe and sock from the affected foot. Dragging the footstool in front of me, I lifted the now red and swollen foot onto it. The frozen peas instantly brought some relief. A second large glass of whisky also helped, this time drunk a little less hastily. What a strange day it had been.

# Epilogue

Momentarily my thoughts return to the last time when I had visited the hospital. Standing in front of the entrance, I looked up to the windows. My eyes focused on the second window to my right, on the third floor. This was the room where Ann spent time recovering from her surgery. It felt as if it were yesterday. A waft of perfume filled my nostrils and I was brought back to my reason for being there again. In my arms, I carried a colourful selection of roses that I had picked from the garden. The grin returned to my face. I felt an overwhelming sense of happiness for the first time since Ann had passed away.

Following the signs, I easily found my way to the corridor and the lift that I was looking for. A short ride in the crowded lift delivered me to the department I was aiming for. Doctors and midwives were busying themselves with whatever their clients had needed. In the middle of the ward was the nurse's station. An efficient looking receptionist was busy typing on a keyboard. Smiling, and in a polite manner, she addressed me and enquired as to my reason for being there. Offering her congratulations, she pointed me in the right direction. Tapping lightly on the door of room number three I opened it.

"Hello in there, can I come in?"

"Of course you can, Granddad. Come and meet your grandson."

Sitting in a bed was my beautiful Lottie, who reminded me of her mother. In her arms, she held her baby. Pete sat by her side displaying the biggest grin on his face; equal only to my own.

"Congratulations to you both. I am so very proud of you."

Lottie ushered me forward to have a closer look at her baby.

"Would you like to hold your grandson?"

Pete lifted the baby from Lottie's arms and placed him in my own. The little baby, that was asleep, now opened his eyes as if to look at me. I placed my finger in his hand and he immediately closed his fingers around it. I could feel the softness of his smooth skin.

"Hello, little one. I'm your granddad."

Pete and Lottie looked on as I spoke reassuringly to my grandson, making promises for his future.

"Dad," Lottie began, "we have decided to name him 'Daniel' after Mum's dad, my grandfather. I know we never got to meet him but I believe he was a good man. Do you think Mum would have liked that?"

Memories came flooding back. The time I had sat in church, waiting for Ann, who was undergoing surgery. I thought about the gentleman that had sat down by my side and had tried to comfort me. The time I fell and injured my ankle. I remembered the gentleman who kindly helped me home.

"I know that she would have been delighted. Welcome, Daniel, welcome to our family."

A knock at the door and Mathew, with Abbie, entered the room.

Baby Daniel was introduced to his uncle and aunt before being returned to his mother for a feed.

How happy we all were. How blessed I felt. On my way home, I decided I would stop and tell the news to Daniel's grandmother.

CPSIA information can be obtained
at www.ICGtesting.com
Printed in the USA
BVHW090958240521
608000BV00012B/2929

9 781788 232975